NO TIME TO MOURN

NO TIME TO MOURN

TIM WOHLFORTH

Quiet Storm Publishing • Martinsburg, WV

All Rights Reserved.

Copyright © 2004 Tim Wohlforth

No part of this book may be reproduced or transmitted in any form or by any means, graphic, electronic, or mechanical, including photocopying, recording, taping or by any information storage or retrieval system, without the permission in writing from the publisher.

Published by Quiet Storm Publishing
PO BOX 1666
Martinsburg, WV 25402

www.quietstormpublishing.com

Cover by : Clint Gaige

ISBN: 0-9749608-2-9

Library of Congress Control Number: 2004105001

This is a work of fiction. Any resemblance to actual events or persons, living or dead, is entirely coincidental.

Printed in the United States of America

"To Joyce, Carl and Bill"

No Time To Mourn

1.

"She's back there," Lori gestured with her head toward a shape bent over a drink at the end of the bar. Hardly human. More like a bundle of black clothes someone had left on the barstool.

I shivered, trying to shake off the dampness of the fogbank I had passed through to get to Big Emma's. As my eyes adjusted to the dim light, the bundle morphed into the semblance of a woman. She was around fifty with high cheekbones and a touch of wrinkle around eyes with dense pupils. Her black suit exuded quality, Nieman-Marcus or Saks. Full red lips that matched bright dyed hair provided the only color. It was as if an artist had begun to colorize her just before she walked out of a frame in a 40's noir movie.

A slight stiffening in her posture suggested she sensed she was being watched. She didn't look up. Just kept staring into her glass.

"See the way she clutches that drink?" I said. "You didn't tell me she's a lush."

Lori looked up from polishing the mahogany surface of the bar. "Didn't used to be. Her name's Susan Henry. Came in here like clockwork every Friday for lunch with her husband, Edward. He'd order a martini. All she ever drank was a Virgin Mary. Then, someone shot Edward. He died in her arms."

"The black clothes. She's still in mourning."

"I can't break her out of it."

Lori returned to her polishing, platinum blond ponytail bobbing up and down. She wore a white turtleneck sweater and a black skirt. A black velvet ribbon held her hair high up on her head. She used to be my lover. Now my best friend. She runs Big Emma's, the Victorian bar on Jack London Square in Oakland, that serves as my office.

"So what can I do? I'm pretty good but I don't bring back the dead. And I'm lousy at consoling. Become tongue-tied. That's your department."

"Keep her alive. She says the same killer is after her now."

Just what I didn't need, Lori dropping a murder case in my lap.

"You know me," I stumbled ahead. "A bit of insurance fraud here. A skip trace there. Murder's for cops."

"She's already seen the cops. They won't help her. She needs you, Jim."

Lori looked up into my eyes, doing that fluttering thing with her eyelashes.

"I'll talk to her, but I'm not promising anything."

"Thanks, Wolf. You'll see."

What I could see was I was going to have a hell of a time talking my way out of this case. I grabbed my drink, Oban's single malt neat, and headed down the bar feeling like a killer on death row who knew the DNA would match. The place was half full. Largely regulars. Two Port of Oakland engineers nodded as I sauntered by. Soon the after-work crowd would pour in.

The interior of Big Emma's was dimly lit by ornate brass lighting fixtures with golden candle-shaped bulbs. A wide mirror in a carved oak frame covered the wall. Dice cups, some with players' names engraved on gold plaques, were stacked on a shelf in front of it. A large brass antique National cash register with monstrous keys stood in the middle. A tantalizing whiff of garlic and cheese floated through the air from the kitchen where cannelloni was being prepared.

I wasn't expecting to hear the truth from Susan. They never tell all. Human nature. Then you've got to use their money to find out the full truth. Part of the game all clients play. Worse. The deeper the trouble clients are in, the more they hold back. I get paid by the hour so I shouldn't complain. Their decision, their bucks. But, sometimes they pay for their reticence with their lives.

Susan didn't look up as I slid onto the stool next to her. Just kept staring into her glass.

"You are?" she asked, as she finally focused on me. At least her glass didn't have to bear the full weight of her intense glare anymore.

"Wolf. Jim Wolf."

"Oh, Lori sent you. It is a pleasure to meet you."

She held out her quivering hand. I grabbed it and received a limp shake. She withdrew her hand from mine immediately. She smelled of lavender and whiskey.

"Lori tells me that someone is trying to kill you."

Susan looked up at me, eyes wide open, as fear broke through her alcoholic fog. "I call him Red."

"Why?"

"He has a red face and drives a red car."

"He's the one who killed your husband?"

"Now he's following me." She shivered. "Bet he's outside right now."

"Just a minute."

I was not about to take Susan at her word. Too much booze leads so often to paranoia. So I figured I better check out her story. I swung off my stool, and made my way out the door.

A thick fog swallowed me up as I entered Jack London Square. I felt a cloud of white pressing in on my face like a feather pillow. Beads of moisture dripped down my forehead. My damp flannel shirt and jeans clung to my body. I turned up the collar on my sports jacket. I heard the dolorous braying of the foghorn off the estuary.

I stopped and looked around. The only light was the shimmering orange glow of Big Emma's behind me. I saw no one. Once again the bleating of the distant foghorn. I trudged on. The tavern's glow dimmed. Then disappeared entirely. I started to check out parked cars. I didn't notice the red Saab until I was almost on top of it. I stopped, backed up a few steps, and strained to make out the license number in the fog. Then I walked casually past the car.

A man sat in the driver's seat, reading the *San Francisco Chronicle* under a dome light. What I could see of his face had a ruddy appearance. He glanced up, eyes glowering through layers of fat, like he was trying to kill me with his glare. Then his lips turned slightly upward at the corners. I looked away but too late. He damned well saw me checking him out. Nothing I could do about it. I hurried down the street and tried to lose myself in the fog.

I went to the end of the block, crossed over, and headed back to Big Emma's. I couldn't see the cars on the opposite side. A car's engine started. The roar of its motor grew louder. Red must have made a U-turn in the middle of the street.

I tried to penetrate the fog. Nothing. Then the glare of headlights pierced the haze. The car bore down upon me. I reached the door of Big Emma's and pulled it open. I hesitated and turned to see which direction Red would go.

Straight at me was his answer. He gunned his engine. The car bashed its way onto the sidewalk. Damn it. The bastard wasn't going to stop. So close that when a puff of fog cleared I could see his face through the windshield. A smirk. The guy was drooling.

2.

I stood frozen in the Saab's headlights for a moment, like a raccoon caught in a tree by a powerful flashlight beam. He couldn't miss me. But I didn't move. Couldn't move. What a stupid way to die. Run over by a fat man who didn't like to be stared at.

I threw myself back into the bar. The car swerved, tires screeched, and the Saab banged back down into the street. Red barreled off toward the warehouse district just past the bar.

I lay on the floor of Big Emma's. A startled crowd of regulars gathered around me. Red had tried to kill me. Just didn't want to smash into the front of Big Emma's. I'd be dead if I had been standing just a few feet further out from the door. I remembered that smile on Red's face when he spotted me. He was entertaining himself. Nothing like running into somebody who liked his work.

Shit. Just what I didn't need, a killer with a hard-on about me. Funny how Lori roped me into things. I'll just talk with Susan, I had told her. Now I was already in over my head. I could identify Red. He knew that. This guy was no amateur. He'd have no difficulty finding out my name and where I lived. I could do it in five minutes if I were in his shoes. I couldn't let this bastard stalk and kill Susan. Then stalk and kill me. I was stuck. A case I couldn't avoid.

"Jim. You okay?"

It was Lori. She broke through the crowd. Cold fog swirled into the open door.

"Just shook up."

"What happened?"

"Your friend Susan's shadow just tried to run me down."

"Sorry for getting you involved."

"Sorry doesn't cover it."

I got up off the floor, brushed myself off. Lori closed the front door. I resumed my perch at the bar. Susan hadn't noticed the commotion by the door. She didn't even look up at me. I took out the small notepad I always carry with me and wrote down the Saab's license number.

"He was out there, but now he's gone," I said to Susan. No sense frightening her more than she already was by telling her about almost getting run down.

"He'll be back."

She seemed startled by her own voice. Her body became rigid. I reached for her hand. She jerked away. I grabbed her icy delicate fingers and got off the barstool. I helped her stand and led her across the room to a quiet booth.

An oil painting of Big Emma hung over us. An enormous, corpulent nude, waves of breast and belly undulating down her body, stretched out on a red velvet settee. Delicate gold leaf legs somehow supported Big Emma's weight. Curly black hair flowed down the nude's back. I loved the expression on her face, defiantly proud of the massive mound of her body. Big Emma was a monument to the joy of human excess from a period when life was short and knowledge of what made it so beneficently absent. So full of vitality. Susan, on the other hand, was preoccupied with death.

"Why are you so certain he's trying to kill you?" I asked.

God knows the bastard was certainly capable of killing.

"Because he tried to kill me before. Edward saved my life by placing his body between me and the bullet."

"You sure Edward wasn't the intended victim of that shooting?"

"Absolutely sure. But the cops think the gunman was after Edward. They think I hired him. Why would I want to kill him? I had both Edward and money. Now I just have money. Look at me."

She had a point.

"Why didn't Red shoot you after killing your husband?"

"The police asked me that. This car stopped in the street just then. Red shot at it. I ran away. Then the cops showed up."

"Let's just say for the moment Edward was the target. Who would have benefited from his death?"

"Me."

"Suppose Red was to succeed in killing you both. Who would benefit?"

"The children."

"What children?"

"Edward's. Edith and Edward, Junior."

We were getting some place. Real suspects.

"So both Edith and Junior might have reason to hire Red."

"Never thought of that."

The bar was filling up. I wasn't sure where they all came from on such a night. Comfort in numbers. I could hear rattling, followed by a loud banging against the bar-top, and then shouts, from an exuberant group playing liars' dice. I leaned toward Susan to hear her better. Startled, she moved back in her seat.

"This man, Red, how long has he been following you?"

"A couple of nights ago, when I got home – I admit I was kind of drunk – there was this red car parked across from the house. Big man sitting in it, reading a paper."

"Red?"

"Think so," she said. Her face became rigid and her eyes opened wide. She was reliving the scene in her mind. "I didn't see him that clearly when he shot Edward. I... I was in shock.

Like a dream. I started thinking back. On other nights along my street, I'd seen that car several times before with the same guy sitting in it. That's when I went to the police."

"And they did nothing?" Oakland's Finest were pretty busy and could be negligent, but this sounded a bit strange.

"They asked me if I was willing to testify in court that this guy was the one who shot Edward. I couldn't. The main cop, a guy called Ollie…"

"I know him."

That's Richard Oliphant and a real bastard he was. He's got it in for me. Hates private eyes, especially the few like me who have never been cops. He was the guy who almost got my license yanked over a homicide investigation. Just my luck that he'd be involved in the Edward Henry case. His partner, Nina Peterson, was different. A doll. One of my best friends.

"He just shrugged his shoulders and said they couldn't do anything for me. I thought they could watch the place and prevent him from killing me."

"You thought wrong."

Cops are reactive not proactive. They saved stakeouts for high-profile drug stings. They claimed it was a matter of manpower. I believed it flowed from their attitude that you're not a homicide case until you're dead. Hell of a way to get their attention.

Might as well get paid for my trouble. And trouble I knew it would be.

"It'll cost you a $1,000 retainer. I'll bill you $90 an hour plus expenses. I account for all time and give receipts on all expenses."

She opened her black Gucci purse and pulled out a roll of bills. All hundreds. She peeled off the top ten and handed them to me. She had more money in that purse than I earn in a good month.

"Always carry that kind of cash?"

"I don't like to feel that I have nothing. I have spent too many years with only change in my pocket."

I said nothing for a few minutes, mulling over what she had told me. All kinds of people committed murder. Still, I couldn't agree with the cops. Didn't picture this sad, screwed-up widow as a killer.

"Don't think Red," she said, "has anything to do with Junior or Edith."

"Why?"

"The way he looked at me when he tried to shoot me and killed Edward instead."

"Why?"

"Why what?"

"If he isn't after you on behalf of Edith and Junior, what is his motivation? Do you come from money?"

"I come from a modest home in Chicago. My maiden name is Kranowsky. The people in my old neighborhood spoke Polish, ate kielbasa and perogis, and belonged to the same local parish. I attended parochial school on a scholarship. I went to the University of Illinois the same way and had to work for my room and board. I taught school in Chicago, then came out here fifteen years ago. I met Henry when I took my students on a tour of his printing plant."

"Red's a professional. He kills for big bucks. Whoever's footing his bill has a damned good reason to have you killed. If it's not the kids, it certainly has nothing to do with perogis. There must be something else."

"I got this photo. My mother, Sara, recently passed away. It was among her things. It shows her standing in front of an adobe building. Somewhere out West. There's a man next to her. It's not my father."

"Could be some old boyfriend, from before she met your father."

"Maybe, but, I feel I knew him. Yet, I don't remember anything about him. Not even his name. He frightens me."

"How about the place? Had you ever been in the West prior to coming to live here in the Bay Area?"

"I'm not sure. I get these visions just before I fall asleep. Images coming from a place between dream and memory. Dust. Heat. Palm trees. Like it's trying to break through. Tell me something. Something important." She shuddered, looked down at her empty glass, and then turned back to me. "Perhaps it's nothing."

Fog. My mind returned for a moment to the white-enshrouded world outside Big Emma's door. The clouds in Susan's mind that blocked out her earliest memories could prove to be more dangerous than the fog outside that protected Red.

"Perhaps it's something. I need to see that picture. I'll be coming up to your place tonight to watch for Red. I'll pick it up then."

She reached for her empty glass. I waved to Lori.

"What do you want?"

"Old Fashioned."

Figured.

3.

The drink came and Susan took a gulp, like she'd been without water in the Mohave for a month. I wrote her address and phone number in my notepad and told her I'd be in touch. She fell silent. I sat taking in her bent black image, like a sketch artist preparing to draw. Double mourning. For her recently departed husband. For her impending death. There was nothing I could do about the first death. But maybe I could prevent the second one. I knew I had to try.

This would be more than a job. I felt I had a personal stake in the outcome of my pending battle with Red. But what stake? I had never met this lady before. I was not into uncontrolled boozing and had little sympathy for drunks. There was always an excuse. Life was one damn big excuse. Each day on my job I saw the weak suffer while the strong take more than their share. But I'd be damned if I was going to drink myself to death.

What was my connection to Susan? I felt a strong empathy that only comes from walking in someone else's shoes. It wasn't the booze. It had to be... her missing past. That's it. The photo. She was haunted by some unknown events that occurred early in her life. So it has always been with me. I was adopted at the age of three. I knew nothing of my early history.

I wondered if she was also adopted. Or for some other reason had an early past that had been hidden from her.

A faint vision formed at the edge of my conscious memory. It began to haunt me as I sipped my whiskey and stared at this black mound opposite me. I saw a woman, huge, hovering over me. Not my mother, that is, not my adopted mother. Frown on her face. Pissed. I had done something wrong. She hit me. Who was she?

Lori kept bugging me to find out more about my birth mother. I knew I could. I was, after all, a PI and pretty damn good at finding people. But I didn't look. Why? I guessed I was afraid of what I might find.

I looked back at Susan. She must share my fears. I became convinced that she knew more about that photo, the place where it was taken, and the man in it than she had told me. But she didn't want to go there. A ghost from the past can be far worse than a predator in the present. As I said, all clients hold back information. Yet she must realize that something out of this past killed her husband and now threatens her life. I considered pressing her for more information, but she was clearly too drunk to string together a coherent sentence. I would have to wait until she was sober again. Perhaps tomorrow morning. I hoped that wouldn't be too late.

I rose from the booth with the remnants of my whiskey, pushed my way through the crowd, and found an empty stool at the bar. A group of longshoremen, all wearing matching jackets with "ILWU" on the back, plowed by carrying on a loud discussion about union politics. A tall black lawyer with city hall connections, who I vaguely knew, slapped me on the back as he moved to his accustomed stool in the rear to join his liars' dice buddies.

No Time To Mourn

Normally at this hour the place began to thin out as customers made their way home for supper and telly with the spouse and kiddies. This night they seemed to have made a collective decision to hang out as long as possible in the hopes that the dense fog would clear.

Lori's brother Joe turned up to handle second shift. She would now have some time for me. Lori's family, the Mazzettis, have owned the joint for three generations. She, Joe, and her mother, Angela, ran the place. Her father, Tony, passed away a few years back.

Lori and I considered ourselves lucky to have saved our friendship after the breakup of our relationship. We have remained closer than most married couples. What did we have in common? Nothing really and that's what made our non-relationship work. She was my connection with other humans. What did I offer in return? I was her private crusade. She was determined to transform me into a social being.

I spent my spare time reading, fiction, nonfiction, newspapers, magazines. I listened to classical music. Mostly baroque and early music. Lori? She talked. When she wasn't in Big Emma's gabbing with customers, she was at home on the phone. Music? Country. Books? Are you kidding?

Lori collected people while I investigated them. I was a voyeur. I listened in on private conversations in restaurants. I was the guy in the corner of a packed living room, back to the wall, sipping my single malt with a sardonic smile on my face, taking in the scene. I didn't run with the pack.

I was sure that my outlook on the world had been influenced by my adoption. I was parachuted into my family. Part of the gang though somehow always apart. Surrounded by people yet alone. Not that I'm complaining. I didn't just pop out. I got picked out. Kind of like shopping at Wal-Mart. The chosen one. I enjoyed being an outsider. Still.

Lori spotted me and made her way toward me. As she approached, she worked the crowd at the bar like a politician, patting a hand here and bussing a cheek there.

"You're really in trouble now, Wolf," Lori said. "Damn it. Be careful. I feel responsible for all this."

"You didn't kill Susan's husband. And you were right. Somebody has to protect that lady."

I gave Lori a rundown on what Susan had told me.

"So what're you going to do?" she asked.

"Chase down the license plate number on the Saab. I'll also stake Susan out. Even if the license plate doesn't lead anywhere, the red Saab will return. Then I'll follow the guy."

"After that?"

"That's the problem. I've got to work the case from two angles."

"What do you mean?"

"I need to go after Red and hope he will lead me to his boss. But I can't assume that, even if I find him, I will be able to connect him to his employer. Professionals know how to keep secrets. The real killer is the person who has hired him. We jail Red and his boss hires a substitute. That's why I need to follow a second track of investigation. Find the employer. I'll investigate the son and daughter. Get that photo from Susan. Check it out."

"If you need late night help, let me know."

Lori sometimes covered a surveillance for me in the middle of the night. I was a day person and began to fade after 1 A.M. That's when Lori clicked in. Probably one more reason why we never worked out a pattern of living together.

"I'll need your help tonight. No way am I going to leave her unwatched."

"Awesome."

A plate of cannelloni I had ordered arrived along with fried zucchini, and fresh Italian bread. I started nibbling on the food. Lori smiled warmly and looked over the crowd at the bar. She

No Time To Mourn

waved to the black lawyer in the rear and winked at one of the longshoremen. Then she turned to me.

"Tonight reminds me of the night after that firestorm in the hills a few years back. Everybody poured in here then as well. And wouldn't leave. Even people whose homes weren't touched. Like we needed to be with each other." Lori waved a long red nail at the door of the bar. "It's a jungle out there."

As if on cue, it opened to admit two customers, neighborhood cops, and buckets of swirling fog. Lori wore her serious look, slight frown, corners of her mouth almost forming a pout.

"Jungle? More like the Okefenokee swamp."

"You know what I mean. You, above all, know that world outside my door. My customers are the walking wounded. They've been out there foraging. Predators hunt them down. A few get eaten up. The rest stagger in here to regroup. We help each other out, listen to stories, and drink a bit. Then, they venture back out into the jungle. Me, I stay here and wait for the hunters and gatherers to return."

"Good, Lori, damn good. Where did you pick up that predator stuff?"

"The Discovery Channel." She paused, her mouth again forming a pout. "You don't take me seriously just because I don't read a lot."

"But I do. Some days I learn more from you in five minutes than a week of reading."

She smiled. It was more than stroking. It was true. Somewhere outside that door, hidden in the fog, lurked a predator far more dangerous than the lions and tigers that used to chew on our ancestors. This predator knew how to use a gun.

"Mind if I have a bite?" Lori asked.

I had eaten only half my cannelloni and hadn't touched the zucchini or bread. I smiled and pushed the plate toward her. Without waiting for my reply she started shoving down the cannelloni as if she hadn't eaten in a week.

"Thanks, I'm ravenous," she said when she came up for air. "I can't get enough of Mama's cooking."

She gave me a slightly guilty glance, like a child that had just gobbled down her family's last piece of pecan pie. Then she took the bread and started soaking up the last remnants of the rich cream sauce.

I raised myself from the barstool and leaned toward her. I could see her miniskirt and shapely long legs that ended up in black shoes with spiked heels. She lifted her head from the plate, turned a cheek, and received her obligatory peck.

"Gotta head home," I said. "Keep an eye on Susan and phone me right after you call her a cab. I want her watched from now on until I find the guy in the red Saab. I'll need you up there later."

"Fabulous."

Susan raised her head from the table as I swung off my stool and walked toward the door. She looked at me, a sad, doomed expression in her eyes. Then she tried to raise one hand. Was she gesturing for me to stop? She muttered something that sounded like "holster." She was really out of it.

I turned up the collar of my sports coat, secured the top button, and involuntarily shivered in anticipation of what I faced on the other side of the door. I stepped out of the bar and into Jack London Square. I felt like I had walked right into the middle of a cotton candy machine, damp fog sticking to me, blinding me, binding me.

No Time To Mourn

4.

    The street was deserted. I crept past Yoshi's restaurant and jazz club. Plate glass windows took up most of a block, exposing customers to perusal by passersby. Couples sat on the floor next to low tables, nibbling on sushi. Slim Asian women with short black hair and red and black kimonos scurried around serving them. McCoy Tyner was playing. A small line of devotees had defied the weather and waited to enter for the eight o'clock set.

    I crossed the street. A tantalizing whiff of popcorn drifted over me. I had smelled the Multiplex before I saw it. I heard the hum of voices and began to make out a scraggly line of restless bodies. The glow of the marquee lights fought back against the fog illuminating eager faces. A ticket line of young people – baggy pants, backward turned caps, Nikes, Gortex sweats – went halfway around the block. Next came Scott's seafood restaurant. A valet parking attendant held open the door of a Mercedes for a stout woman with blue-white hair, wearing a pink, sequined gown. She held up an umbrella. A lot of good it would do her.

    Pockets of light, noise, and crowds disappeared. I stopped by a railing for a moment, engulfed in darkness and fog. I could hear the lapping of the water against the hulls of a hundred private yachts, while halyards slapped the aluminum masts. The more I stared into the fog the less I could see. A strange hue, almost yellow, unnatural.

I sensed Red out there. Watching. Waiting. Damn it, I was more pissed than frightened. To the extent that there was a place for me in this crazy world – and I had some big doubts on that subject – it was here in Oakland, at the bottom of Broadway, on the edge of the estuary across from the island of Alameda. I was not about to be hounded out of my turf.

I stepped onto the deck of *Sea Wolf*, the thirty-seven foot sloop I called home. I unlocked the hatch, slid it back, removed the two boards that sealed the opening, and descended the stairs through the companionway. A bell rang. I grabbed the phone, tucked away in my nav. That's a small built-in table with drawers where the captain — me — works on his charts and tide tables when sailing. I heard breathing and then a click. Wrong number. Or was it?

I thought again about Red. He could have followed me from Big Emma's. I didn't spot him but what could I see in the fog? He tried to kill me once with his car. Next time it would be with a bullet.

I climbed back up the companionway stairs, pushed open the hatch cover, and looked around. In the distance I could hear the relentless bleating of the foghorn off the estuary. Every ninety seconds. My head pounded in synchronization. It was as if the estuary mourned for Susan. The fog contributed a damp shroud to cover her almost cold body. But she wasn't dead. It was my job to stop Red, to save Susan. Maybe even encourage her to get rid of that hideous black outfit. Swear off the juice. Come alive again. Too soon to mourn. I saw nothing, but I could only see a few feet in any direction.

I climbed back down into the cabin and checked on Monty, my pet python. I kept her in a glass reptile tank that

No Time To Mourn

took up about half of the quarterberth – that's the bed in the aft of the boat. Two beady eyes greeted me. Her tongue flicked out. About as warm a greeting as Monty can offer.

I wasn't really the pet type. Don't like something furry rubbing against my leg and purring. Or slobbering all over me, licking my face and covering me with smelly saliva. Monty, to her credit, did neither. We respected each other's space.

I didn't actually choose Monty as a pet. I got stuck with her. It was all Sheila's fault, one of the many Lori had set me up with. Sheila left her with me. Told me Monty was a male. It's kind of hard to tell about gender with snakes. When Monty got sick one day — visualize a very limp rope — I found out from the vet that she was actually a female Burmese python.

Sheila worked as a belly dancer at the Greek place, Never On Sunday, down on Broadway. Also gave lessons. I must say she had a most remarkable belly. Fabulous muscles. I had moved into her loft in a warehouse area a couple of blocks up the street from Big Emma's.

One day I went to the Greek joint to watch Sheila. This nerdy guy with thick glasses and a gray flannel suit kept stuffing hundred dollar bills into Sheila's crotch. Got to admit it, I was jealous. Sheila explained between sets that this was an old Egyptian custom. I didn't feel any better. Sheila was Jewish and from Brooklyn. The guy wasn't Egyptian either, not even Greek. He was a WASP from Seattle. Worked for Microsoft.

The combination of Microsoft and hundred dollar bills in the crotch was too much for Sheila to resist. She took off for Seattle with him. Said she'd come back for Monty as soon as they got settled. That was three years ago. I recently heard she's pregnant with her second kid.

The vet had told me Monty would eventually grow to twenty or thirty feet and could be as thick as a telephone pole. A seven foot constrictor was dangerous enough. Could kill a man. I was not about to wait until Monty reached twenty feet for Sheila to return.

Tim Wohlforth

I developed a plan in my head. One way to recover my very frayed nerves. If Sheila didn't return before Monty grew too big for the boat, I'd put her in a crate and ship her by special courier to a certain address in Redmond, Washington. The world would never miss one less computer programmer.

I decided I might as well take some action related to the case while I waited for Lori to call. I would start with a call to Nina Peterson, Oakland's only African American female detective, and my good friend. She answered the phone.

"It's Wolf. I need a favor."

"What else is new?"

"Bring the kids by the boat and Monty and I'll baby-sit while you and Duane take in a flick."

Duane's the husband. He also works for Oakland PD and readily admits she's smarter and tougher than he is. Now that's a nice guy!

"You'll feed 'em to that damned cobra of yours."

"Python. Her jaw won't stretch wide enough to get a kid's head in. A Chihuahua maybe."

"Great! Only a leg or foot! What can I do you for?"

"Information on a license number."

"I'm home."

"But you can make a call for me. Just a chance there's some warrants outstanding, or it's hot. Then it would be in that computer bank of yours. Wouldn't have to check DMV."

"I'll make one call."

I read off to her the license number from my notepad.

"Phone as soon as I can. But, it could take time, Jimmie."

She hung up. Jimmie. She's the only one who calls me that. Even my mother, after a lot of pleading on my part, went over to Jim when I became a teenager. Now most people just call me Wolf, which suited me fine. I suspected Nina wanted to place me on the same level as her children. She liked to be in charge.

I could do nothing but wait for Lori or Nina to call. I put on one of my favorite CDs, Yo Yo Ma playing Bach's *Suites for*

No Time To Mourn

Unaccompanied Cello, and curled up on the berth. Usually soothes me. Not this night. I was still troubled about the hang-up phone call.

I was really getting into a funk. The slapping of the halyard against the mast, which usually lulls me to sleep, irritated me. Yo Yo Ma paused between suites. I thought I heard faint footsteps on the floating dock. I wouldn't have noticed if I hadn't been so keyed up. Yo Yo Ma started sawing away on a new suite. I pressed the pause button on the CD player and listened again. Yes. Footsteps.

I grabbed my .38, a Smith & Wesson Bodyguard Airweight, from the drawer under the nav table. The five-shot double action revolver was perfect for my line of work. With a two-inch barrel and weighing only fourteen and a half ounces, it was easy to conceal. I stuck the gun into my belt and threw on a black turtleneck sweater to cover it up. I crept up the companionway stairs and peeked out of the opening under the hatch cover. Nothing.

I shoved the cover all the way back and hoisted myself onto the deck in one smooth motion. I heard a faint ping and a splintering sound. A gunshot, damn it. Red had a silencer. Close. The bullet had struck just inches from my head. I dropped flat on the deck. He could see me. Maybe a special sight on his gun or night vision goggles. But where the hell was he? No doubt waiting for me to move. Then he'd shoot again. Next time he wouldn't miss. Hired to hunt down Red, I had become the hunted.

Why was he so damned determined to pop me? I could think of only one reason. He planned to off Susan that night. With me dead, there would be no one to identify him. He would just take off and that would be the end of it. I couldn't just lie there waiting for him to finish me off. I had to get him before he got me and then Susan. I had no choice.

I heard steps heading down the floating dock toward the gangway to the shore. Must be Red. I lifted myself up from the deck, hopped onto the dock, and ran toward the sound. I tripped on some rope. Shit. I pulled myself up and plowed forward. The gangway lay ahead somewhere. There. I saw its outline, then the shore itself.

A dark phantasm, looking like a giant gargoyle, separated itself from the fog. Red was wearing a black suit. He stood on the dock ten feet away. The bastard had been waiting for me as I clumsily – noisily — ran down the dock. He stared right at me, his gun in hand. He grinned like a little boy let loose in a toy store with papa's credit card.

I grabbed my revolver out from under my belt. Too late. Red had raised his gun – small, long, thin muzzle, a scope – as if he had all the time in the world. He had me. No way could he miss.

5.

Red fired as a swell from a passing boat rocked the dock. I felt a blow against my shoulder. Like somebody had hit me with a two by four. That boat saved my life. I wouldn't get another break. I dropped flat on the dock as he squeezed the trigger again. I rolled over to the edge and dropped into a tethered dingy. Another ping. His bullet smashed into the dock exactly where I had been seconds before.

Hoping the little boat's hull would protect me, I pulled my .38 out from my belt, and aimed directly at the scumbag. My shoulder burned like someone placed a hot branding iron on it. I grew dizzy. My hand shook. I fired and missed.

Red turned and ran toward the gangway. Each foot thudded on the floating dock, causing it to sway. He melted into the damned fog. The bastard didn't mind plugging an unarmed elderly man on a quiet street or taking shots at me in the dark, but he didn't have much taste for a one-on-one shootout.

I crawled out of the boat. I ripped off my shirt and pressed it against my wound to staunch the flow of blood. Holding my gun in the other hand, I staggered after him. The dock rocked under my feet as a large vessel passed on the estuary. My balance shifted. I gripped the bulkhead to steady myself, swaying over the water between the shore and the floating dock. The gun fell from my hand and bounced on the planks. I grabbed the revolver just before it rolled into the water.

I raised myself and started forward. A dark specter rose out of the fog. Red. He was moving swiftly up the gangway. I was almost on top of him. He had yet to notice me. I heard a deep moan blasted by a passing tug.

I stopped and drew a bead with my .38 right square in the middle of his back. It was like a turkey shoot. Damn it. I couldn't steady my hand. Then the wake of the tug hit the float I was standing on. I fired. The bullet missed the bastard by inches.

Red heard the explosion, glanced back, and took off. I had never seen a fat man move so fast. Shoving the gun back into my belt, I dashed after him. No time to think. I stumbled onto an empty sidewalk and stared directly into an impenetrable fogbank. I heard movement but couldn't see a damned thing.

The blast of a whistle. The beam of a headlight. An Amtrack train pierced the fog just the other side of the parking lot. Red was silhouetted in the light. I took careful aim, holding the gun in two hands. Finally, I could steady my hands. Had him. I fired just as he threw himself in front of the engine. I figured that was the end of him. If my bullet missed, the train would finish him off. I heard no scream nor did I see a body flying through the air. I had figured wrong.

I drove myself head-on toward the locomotive. Had no plan. All I could think of was that bastard Red. Had to stop him. Kill him. I forced myself to stop as the behemoth rolled past me. I could have reached out and touched the cold steel.

The locomotive slowed, massive brakes screeched as they gripped iron wheels. A blast of compressed air knocked me onto the macadam. Scraped my damned knee. I forced myself up and stood transfixed as the cars crawled by. Not being Superman, I couldn't leap over the damned thing.

Passengers sat comfortably in plush seats, reading novels, snoozing, chattering to themselves, oblivious to the drama outside. No one bothered to look out the window. What was

No Time To Mourn

there to see? Just fog. One exception. A young girl with long straight black hair, pink dress with white lace trimming, pressed her nose against the window. Her brown eyes opened wide, like she was standing in front of F.A.O. Schwartz on Christmas Eve. She spotted me and smiled. A fellow voyeur.

When the last car crawled by, freeing my view, Red had disappeared. Quiet descended once again on the Jack London Square waterfront. Patches of fog, like puffs of smoke from an antique steam engine, swirled around me. I drifted back in the direction of my boat, energy drained from my body. My shoulder was aflame with pain. Had to make it back to the *Sea Wolf*. Patch myself up. Think for a change.

I almost tripped over a couple sitting on a bench necking. They didn't even look in my direction. Disco music sounded in the distance. I turned and looked out over the estuary. I could see nothing. The music grew louder. A glow of light, the chatter of couples talking, an occasional high laugh floated toward me as the party boat made its way down the estuary. Blasts from that damned foghorn ricocheted through my skull every ninety seconds. I counted the time between brays.

I climbed onto the *Sea Wolf's* deck and carefully lowered myself through the hatch. Almost got the bastard. Another way to look at it was that he shot me and almost finished me off. I was not about to catch this fellow on adrenaline alone.

I cleaned my shoulder with antiseptic. Luckily just a surface wound, as I had no time for hospitals and doctors. Needed to be ready to stake out Susan. But I had to get some rest. I turned off the cabin light and lay down on my berth, a comfortable double bed in the fo'c's'le. Every now and then the faint glow from a passing vessel shimmered through the portholes giving the interior teak woodwork a rich reddish color. The blue curtains, with their corny little white anchors, fluttered from the slight breeze coming in the main hatch. I dozed.

The phone rang. Nina. I really needed to talk with her.

"Where you be?" she asked. "I called fifteen minutes ago and there was no answer."

"I've been running around the docks getting shot at. That's were I've been."

I told Nina the whole story starting with Susan.

"Your description of the fat dude's not much to go on."

"But I gave you his license number."

"You said your shooter drove a red Saab? The plates are on the hot list all right, registered to a green Accord. The owner reported them stolen two days ago."

"Great!"

I had expected something like that. Still a guy can hope for a break now and again.

"I'm afraid we're dealing with a professional criminal of some kind. That's what I get paid to handle. I want you to stay put. I'll call the night duty desk and have the patrolman for the Jack London Square area keep an eye on your boat when he makes his rounds. We'll send out a crime team in the morning and retrieve that bullet from the side of your boat."

"Don't want you gouging my hull."

"Fussy. The guy could have killed you, you dig?"

"But what about Susan?"

"I'll tell the night duty sergeant about her, too. I'm afraid that the department hasn't the bodies to put a patrolman on her door any more than on yours."

"Better than last time. She says she told you guys about Red but you refused to help her."

"That was Ollie." Nina didn't get along with her partner Richard "Ollie" Oliphant. "But he did have his reasons."

"Such as?"

"He and I were assigned to that Edward Henry shooting. We were convinced she set it all up."

"So why didn't you prosecute her?"

"No evidence, but it was so fishy. Married six months, the husband gets shot, and suddenly the bird's worth millions."

"Millions?"

"The estate's been assessed at five million dollars. The way I figured it the guy in the red Saab's the professional she hired to bump off the husband. Then she got tight and didn't want to pay him off. There's another possibility."

"I know. Maybe she paid him off and he's come back to shake her down for more. He's stalking her until she comes through."

"You got it, man. In that case he's trying to scare her, not kill her. At least not until he gets his money."

I may have gotten in the way of a lot of dough. Could be in more danger than Susan. Monty pulled her wedge-shaped head away from the rest of her tightly coiled body and stared at me. Tongue flicking. Her striking pose. She knew I was wounded. Wanted to help. And they say snakes have no heart.

"You hire a scumbag and that's what you get," Nina continued. "When she came in again, Ollie figured not much we could do for the lady unless she fessed up."

"Doesn't fit with the Susan I interviewed."

"Here we go again. You go by your instincts and, much of the time, the seat of your pants. I go by facts. I've heard too many stories in my life from the time I was a kid growing up in the West Oakland projects. If I believed everything I was told, I would have been pregnant at the age of thirteen."

"You must have been cute."

"You better believe it."

"Look, I respect the way you investigate. I can't remember anyone putting anything over on you, Nina. It's just that sometimes…"

"You get these feelings."

"I can't shake my conviction that Susan is in real trouble that isn't of her own making. Otherwise why is this Red asshole so determined to kill me?"

"A nice white guy like you? You do have a point. This Red dude is a definite fact. Hate to cut you short, Honey, but I've got to get the troops out of the hot sun."

"Hot sun?"

"Well, away from the TV. It's time to put the kiddies to bed and I can't leave everything to Duane."

"Give 'em all my love."

I turned off the lights aft so that Monty could enjoy some nighttime slithering and pressed the pause button on the CD player to release Yo Yo. I dozed off again.

The phone rang. This time Lori.

"Joe's called a cab for Susan. She was definitely in her cups. Funny thing."

"What?"

"Just before she asked Joe to call the cab she got a phone call."

"Shit. That happen often?"

"Never. Joe was the one who answered the call for her. He said she muttered something about an appointment. That's when she told him she wanted the cab right away."

"Could be Red or an accomplice setting her up. Damn it Lori, it will happen tonight."

"When do you want me?"

"You better come on up right away. I'm a little weak."

"Still shaking from Red's attempt to run you down?"

"Worse. Ran into him again. He shot me in the shoulder."

"I'm coming right over. Get you to a hospital."

"Can't leave Susan unwatched. He's going to try to kill her tonight."

I hung up before she could argue any further. I wondered who had called Susan. Could have been Red. But somehow I doubted it. All I had gotten out of Red on the phone was heavy breathing. Too smart to have someone hear his voice. An accomplice? Red seemed the type to work alone. Like me. That left his employer. She was being killed by someone she knew.

No Time To Mourn

Edith? Junior? Yes, both fitted. Had to get up to Susan in time to save her and then ask her about the phone call.

Maybe I'd wrap up this case tonight. If I was lucky. If not, I'd be hunting down Susan's murderer.

I stuck my gun back into my belt, lifted the hatch cover cautiously, and slipped out into the fog. I hopped on the dock, withdrew the gun from my belt, and took off the safety. Holding my gun in my one good hand I made my way slowly up the floating dock toward the gangway.

Something brushed my leg. Instinctively, I fired. Almost hit my foot. Goddamn rat.

6.

Fog rarely makes its way up to the higher and richer regions of Oakland. That night was the exception. The fog's fingers had penetrated Crocker-Highlands. Streetlights were transformed into fuzzy orange balls. Wisps of fog chased each other slowly along the street. At one moment the air was clear, the next dense as in front of Big Emma's. Damp and sticky. This was not going to be an easy surveillance.

I found Susan's house with little difficulty. The formal gray two-story monster dominated Mandana Avenue. Set back from the street, the place featured a well-manicured lawn and sculptured shrubs that made it look like the setting for a Henry James novel. Similarly pretentious mansions, almost as large, lined the rest of the quiet, curving, oak-shrouded street. Susan had married well.

I had beaten Lori there. Didn't need her immediately. However, I was worried about the long haul. The wound had weakened me. I couldn't afford to doze off in the middle of this surveillance. I would wake up to a dead Susan.

I positioned my black '97 Taurus between two streetlights across from the house's entrance. Tauruses are good surveillance cars. One of the most popular models in the country. Who would notice an extra Taurus parked by the curb or following along in traffic?

No Time To Mourn

I couldn't see much because of the fog, but then I couldn't be seen either. The porch light was on. Probably connected to a timer. Helped a little bit.

I enjoyed surveillance work. I placed "Portrait" by the Anonymous 4 in my CD player. Haunting *a capella* medieval music. Pure voices. Somehow the music seemed appropriate for Susan. Alone now. Hunted by an anonymous killer. I poured out some strong French roast in the cup end of my thermos, and prepared for a long evening.

I was getting settled in when a Yellow Cab pulled up in front of the house. The driver, a gangly longhaired fellow, went around to the passenger side of the cab, opened the door, and helped Susan out. She stumbled. Then the two disappeared completely into the fog. The glare from the porch light fell on them as they emerged from the fog. He had picked her up and held her like a little child. He seemed to be used to the duty. Had her house key in his hand. He opened the door and carried her in.

He returned in about five minutes, got back into his taxi, and lit what looked more like weed than a Marlboro. Sat there for awhile getting stoned. Then started his engine and lumbered unsteadily down the street. I made a mental reservation to specify no tall longhairs should I need to order a Yellow Cab in the future.

Finally peace. It was a quiet night. Only a slight breeze stirred the puffs of fog. The Anonymous 4 had made it to Hildegarde von Bingen. The music of this 12th Century nun and mystic struck me as richly sensuous. Sort of like Middle Ages blues. Denied the temporal pleasures, Hildegarde did her best to get what she could out of spiritual lust. Uplifting.

I heard a car slowing down. It was Lori's white Trans-Am. Admittedly not the world's best surveillance vehicle, but helping me out was only a sideline for her. She parked behind my Taurus, clambered out of her car and ran toward me. She wore red and white checkered formfitting slacks, a tight red sweater, black denim vest, shoulder bag and sandals. Her platinum blond hair was held high up on her head in a ponytail by a red ribbon. Who else would bother to put on a bow to match a sweater when going out on a stakeout? Got to admit she looked fabulous, though not necessarily inconspicuous. I opened the door for her. She bopped in and gave me a big hug.

"Ow."

"Sorry I forgot. Where are you shot?"

"Shoulder."

"You shouldn't be here."

"I have to be here."

"Want me to take over now?" she asked.

"I've got to be here. Your job is to keep me from nodding off."

"I'll talk."

"That's what I figured."

I reached over and gave her a kiss on the cheek. I heard the rumble of a motorcycle coming up the street.

"There."

I grabbed my binoculars and lowered the window. A gorgeous Harley, riderless, the headless horseman. Then, as a wisp of fog blew away, I spotted a small person, dressed in black leather with a black helmet, crunched over the bike. She deftly swung the brute of a machine between two parked cars, bounced over the curb and onto the sidewalk, slamming on the brakes when the front tire was a foot from Susan's door. The driver and bike were silhouetted under the porch light. I could make out the license number with the help of my binoculars. Wished I had the night vision kind. She took off her helmet, revealing short strawberry blond hair. A quite attractive she.

I handed the binoculars to Lori and asked, "Who the hell is that?"

"Edith, Susan's stepdaughter. She's a lesbian biker."

"What is she doing here?"

"Maybe she's the one who made the phone call. Trying to get money out of Susan."

No Time To Mourn

Edith cut the engine, banged on the door, and shouted, "Susan! I know you're in there. Open up this damned door."

No sound from inside. She tried the knob and walked right in. The dumb taxi driver had forgotten to lock the door. The hallway was dimly lit. The light must have been coming from a room in the back of the house. I tried to see what was happening inside, but my angle was wrong and the fog too thick. No noise. The silence spooked me. Suppose Susan wasn't being shot, just strangled or stabbed? Something must be going on in there. I prepared to open my door and head for the house to investigate.

I heard pounding feet from inside the house. Our young woman ran out the door, jumped on the Harley and, throwing the entire weight of her little body down on one foot, gave it a professional kick start. The engine roared, wheels spun, digging up some of Susan's lawn, and she was off.

"I'm following her," I said. "You're in charge. If Red turns up call me on your cell phone."

Lori opened the door and headed for the Trans-Am. I turned on the engine and swung the Taurus out in the street. I gunned the engine and twisted on down Mandana until I picked up Edith's taillight. I wasn't worried about being spotted. Just hung back enough to be absorbed by the fog. We wound ourselves down the road toward the bay. The fog got thicker. She was preoccupied with getting some place very fast. She was determined to put as much distance as she could between herself and Susan's house. I wondered why.

I clocked her at seventy charging down curvy Mandana toward Lakeshore Avenue. She ran the light by the freeway. I found myself on the road that snakes along the shore of Lake Merritt. I could barely make out the string of tiny lights that hung from lampposts at the water's edge. I followed the glow in the fog from the taillight on her motorcycle.

My cell phone rang. Shit. I reached to pick it up. Just when things were getting interesting.

"What is it?" I asked Lori.

Tim Wohlforth

"Red showed up just when I was going to check on Susan. I'm hiding behind a juniper bush right now. Don't think he saw me. He's heading for the front door, holding something that could be a gun."

"Don't go after him. I'll be right there."

I slowed down just enough to make a U-turn. Then barreled back to Susan's place. I parked in front of the house, opened the glove compartment, took out my .38, and clicked off the safety. I was prepared to plug the bastard and determined not to miss this time. I hopped out and started tearing toward the door. A figure leapt out from behind a bush and ran toward me. I swung toward the object, raising my gun, and began to squeeze the trigger.

"Don't shoot. It's me."

Lori, for God's sake.

"Never, never do that. Shout out first, then approach."

I had no time to discuss the matter further. Had to get into that house. I ran blindly toward the dim halo of light pouring out of the open front door. I tripped, banging my knee against some damned concrete lawn ornament. Cupid. I got up, reoriented toward the light, dashed across the remaining strip of lawn, jumped over a flowerbed, and landed on the front steps.

Red exploded out of the door opening, broad shoulders, huge torso, and banged into me with one hand held out stiffly like a football player. Bet the guy played college ball years back. He held his gun in the other hand.

I fell to the ground, gasping for air. Landed on my shoulder. Opened up the wound. I could feel blood dripping down my arm. God my shoulder ached. For a moment I couldn't move. Then I forced myself up and staggered after him, one hand pressed against the wound, the other holding my revolver.

I reached him just as he grabbed the Saab's door. He swung the car door wide open, smashing the curved red metal into my side. It hit my ribs with the force of a pile driver.

No Time To Mourn

Knocked the wind completely out of my lungs. I crashed to the pavement beside the curb, landing on my back. A new piercing pain joined my aching shoulder. He yanked the door closed, started the engine, shifted into gear, and took off like a goddamned rocket. The Saab's back wheel missed my leg by half an inch.

I rolled over on my stomach, winced as my bruised ribs hit the macadam, steadied my gun with my one good hand, and fought to clear my head so I could focus. Couldn't see the car in the fog but I knew where it was. Where it had to be. I got off one shot. I'm sure I hit the back of the Saab. Finally one for me.

Lori ran up to me. She was an easy target for Red.

"Damn it," I yelled. "The guy's got a gun. Down!"

I yanked her arm. She fell next to me. I threw my arm around her and held her tight, shielding her with my body. Big mistake. I moaned and involuntarily pushed her away. My ribs.

"Jim, you're hurt."

"I know, but I got the bastard. Hit his car."

I had no chance to continue the discussion. I had expected Red would take off around the bend in that Saab of his. I figured wrong. I heard his car slow down and stop, then a door open. I couldn't see a damned thing.

A flash of light and that goddamned ping again. His bullet smashed into the pavement inches from my head. I fired back. My shot went astray. My gun fell out of my grip. Somehow I picked it back up and fought to focus my vision to get off another shot.

The fog moved in suffocating me, forcing its clammy way into my mouth, my nose, my eyes, my ears. The mist entered my brain. Darkness.

Tim Wohlforth

7.

Blurry vision, throbbing head, but I could see. The fog around me, as well as in my mind, had cleared. No Red. I must have been out for no more than a minute. In the distance I heard the roar of a car racing away.

Lori floated in front of me, wisps of fog clung to her blond hair and enveloped her whole body. Looked like my concept of an angel when I was eight years old. I was a precocious kid and liked my angels a bit on the sexy side.

"Your shoulder's bleeding again. I'm sure you got a broken rib or two as well. Got to get you an ambulance."

"Later. Must check Susan. Help me up."

I was still short of breath, finding it difficult to speak. Lori put one arm around me just below my shoulders and supported my weight. She was surprisingly strong. I'm not heavy for my height. Still a solid one hundred and sixty-five. I felt like huge stones had been tied to my legs. I forced each foot forward and struggled to keep my eyes focused. I had a massive, but dull, headache. Dizziness. I knew greater clarity would bring greater pain. We staggered toward the gray house like Siamese twins. Lori stumbled on the steps. We almost fell. I was no help at all.

The door stood wide open before us, exposing a long dark hallway with dim light at the end. I allowed her to drag me

No Time To Mourn

inside. I pushed her hand away and tried to walk on my own. A mistake. My legs dissolved into Jell-O, and I was overcome with dizziness and nausea. I felt myself float toward the floor. Blurry image of Lori's face. Then blackness.

"Jim! Jim! Wake up, Goddamn you. I love you!"

I awoke to find my head in Lori's lap. She had taken her denim vest off and was pressing it against my shoulder. That vest must have cost her a fortune, and the blood would ruin it. Talk about sacrifice.

"Now you lie here for a sec," Lori said. "I'll see if I can find Susan."

She left me and headed toward the room at the end of the hall. I struggled to my feet, holding Lori's vest against my shoulder. I staggered down the hall, drawn toward the shimmering ghostly illumination emanating from its end. The price I paid for a return to full consciousness was almost unbearable pain. My rib cage, where the door struck, ached, but the center of my misery was the reopened wound in my shoulder.

I heard a scream from the room at the end of the hall. Someone or something hit the floor. Then a moan.

I forced my way down the hall, step by painful step, and entered a room filled with a flickering cold green luminescence. Seemed to be a study. Where was Lori? Susan? I forged ahead and almost stumbled over Lori. She lay flat on her stomach, face to the side, checkerboard legs as well as arms splayed apart, forming a swastika on the polished wood floor. Her sandals and shoulder bag were entangled in a small rug. Tears flowed from her blue eyes, mascara stained her rouged cheeks, ponytail stuck straight out across the floorboards like a noose. It's not easy for Lori to look terrible, but she sure was making an effort.

"She's dead," she said.

"But you? What happened?"

"I was crying so much I couldn't see. Guess I tripped."

I knelt down beside her and placed her head in my lap, our roles reversed. I leaned over and kissed her stained cheek.

"Sorry," she said. "I'm no help. You're the one hurt."

I placed her vest, now soaked with my blood, under her head. I rose to look for Susan's body. Blood oozed down my arm. For some stupid reason all I could think of was that I was messing up Susan's floor. I must have been a sight.

Lori stood up and handed her vest back to me. I pressed it against the wound with one hand. She made an effort to hold me, but she shivered. I tucked my free arm around her and tried to stop her shaking. I couldn't stop myself from shivering in rhythm with her. Contagious. We were no good to anyone, not even each other. After a minute I pulled myself together.

"Where is she?"

Lori didn't answer. Instead, she took hold of my arm and steered me across the room. Dark wood panels halfway up the walls, then white plaster. Stained beams in the ceiling. A large oak desk dominated the end of the room. The only illumination came from a brass antique reading lamp with a green glass shade on the desk.

A black shape lay sprawled under the lamp. Lori froze in place, like one of those living sculptures who perform at Fisherman's Wharf. I freed myself from her grip, moved forward and stared down on Susan's dead body. Her head rested on its side on top of a green blotter, dyed red hair taking on a ghastly purple color under the emerald rays of the light. One hand lay limp on the blotter, holding a gold-framed picture. The other hand hung loosely at her side, like a puppet whose pieces sprung in place when you pulled the strings.

A bullet had pierced her temple, leaving a clean, surgically precise, hole. Little blood. Her blank eyes held me in their grip like Red's headlights earlier that evening. Was she accusing me of letting her down? She had a right to do so.

No Time To Mourn

What had those pupils seen during her last moments of life? Had to be Red pointing a gun at her. Who hired Red? Susan couldn't help now. Or could she? The photo. Her last living act had been to grip that photo.

"She was really so sweet." Lori said. She stood by my side.

All I could think of was the way Susan looked the last time I saw her, defenseless, imploring me to help her. Mourning for her husband. Mourning for herself. I hadn't succeeded in protecting her. Somehow, some way, I had to nail the bastard who had killed her.

"I couldn't stop the killer."

"You tried your best. That's why you're such a mess."

I was having trouble concentrating. So far all I had was questions. No answers.

"My vest's not stopping your bleeding. I'm calling 911. Not taking any argument. Then I'll fix you up."

She pulled her cell phone out of her slacks' pocket and punched in 911. I was amazed she could work a phone with those long, bright-red nails. She called for an ambulance for me.

"I'm finding a bathroom so I can clean you up and put some antiseptic on that gash."

She took her vest back, and handed me a fistful of Kleenexes. She gave me a kiss on the forehead and was off. My shoulder was competing with my side to see which could hurt worse. Just standing there was driving me crazy. Had to do something to get my mind off the pain. I decided on a closer look at Susan and her desk.

An open Gucci bag lay next to Susan's hand. I wiped the blood off my hands. Then I spread open the purse so I could see all the way to the bottom. The roll of hundred dollar bills was missing. Hard to believe she had been killed for the money in her purse. Pocket change when compared to what her estate was worth. Still, somebody took the money. Red getting a down payment for his work? Edith? The cab driver?

Tim Wohlforth

I pried open Susan's delicate fingers. Still slightly warm. I looked into those vacant eyes as if to apologize. I knew she didn't like to be touched. I took the picture she held so tightly and placed it under the light on the desk. A young, strikingly beautiful copy of Susan stared up at me. The woman in the faded black and white photo wore a tailored dark suit, a snood and a pillbox hat. I looked over at Susan. So alike. All that was missing was the pillbox hat.

Susan's mother Sara clutched the arm of a handsome man in a World War II army uniform. Glacial rectangular face. Determined to succeed in an uncertain postwar world. At what cost? At whose expense?

An adobe building with yucca trees in front dominated the background. Definitely not Chicago. More like the Central Valley, San Diego, Arizona. As I looked down upon her lifeless body, I promised her to find out its meaning.

I knew I would never see the damned thing again after the cops arrived. The photo would go into an evidence bag and no one outside of the department would be allowed anywhere near it until a trial or possibly during the disclosure procedure. Susan wanted me to have that picture.

Lori returned with a steaming washcloth, a towel, and a bottle of some horrible looking substance that I knew would sting.

I heard the wail of sirens in the distance.

"You've got to help me," I said.

I found a manila envelope in one of the drawers of the desk. I shoved the picture into it, licked the flap and sealed the envelope.

"Just bury this in your purse. Remember the cops have no right to look in your purse without getting a search warrant."

Lori did as I said. Then she wiped off my bleeding shoulder with a hot cloth. It felt like she was scraping my shoulder with razor blades. The worst was yet to come. The antiseptic hit me like dozens of Africanized honeybees

No Time To Mourn

determined to destroy this white man for good. I staggered. Lori led me to a chair at the other end of the room.

I wondered, not for the first time, why in the world I chose this particular line of work. The pay was pretty spotty, and there were times when someone decided to use my body to perfect his torturing skills. Training for a position in the Bosnian Army.

Then I raised my head, and my eyes fixated on the small, lifeless body of Susan sprawled across that huge desk. The lady in mourning, dressed for her own funeral. The ghoulish purple hue of her hair. I felt as I had when I had first met her earlier that day. Time warp. She had stepped out of another era. Not equipped to handle our times. Destroyed by forces she could not comprehend. Forces I had to identify. One more victim of evil. I knew why I was a private eye.

8.

The ambulance's siren blasted away. The driver was taking no chances in the dense fog. I lay on a stretcher, face up, staring into the nonchalant eyes of an all-business female paramedic. Each bump sent a piercing pain through my body. They sure had a lot of potholes on Oakland's streets. I couldn't help wincing.

"Need something for the pain?" The young woman asked.

"How about morphine?"

I figured I'd give it a shot. I'm not a druggie, but right then I wouldn't have minded a touch of euphoria.

"Coming up."

The morphine helped. The pain subsided and I fell into a dreamy state. Susan had touched off in me buried feelings, distant memories. She was hounded by a past she didn't know, a past expressed in that photo she clutched as she died. How well I understood the emptiness created in those robbed of their earliest memories.

I found myself replaying in my mind my recent trip to Connecticut to visit my adopted parents. My mother had insisted. She had something to tell me.

It was a crisp, cool, but sunny, fall day. The hill behind my parents' home in New Canaan, Connecticut was covered with the skeletons of trees. The green of summer, and the bright

No Time To Mourn

reds and yellows of early fall, were gone. Gave the place a stark forbidding look. Naked trees waited for the soft white cover of snow. My parents hadn't been able to keep the place up as they once had. Dead leaves smothered the dying yellowed grass of the back lawn.

I watched my mother, now eighty years old, digging in the flowerbed. A pile of uprooted bulbs stood beside her. They were destined to spend the winter in the root cellar under the house. Behind her rambled a low stone wall, constructed in the colonial period, rocks dispersed by time. In the distance a nine-foot tall chicken wire fence of more recent vintage surrounded the vegetable garden. Designed to keep deer out, it looked like a displaced-persons' camp. The fenced-in area lay fallow. The deer couldn't care less.

"You should be inside resting, Mother."

"I haven't got long, but I'll be damned if I'll spend my last days cooped up in the house." She paused and removed my father's worn work gloves. "How's your private eye business? I was one hell of a crime reporter in the old days. Bet I could still give you some pointers."

"I'm sure you could."

My mother was not short on self-confidence. The walls of her study were plastered with clippings from the famous murder trials she had covered. Axe murderers, rapists, lover's lane butchers, devil worshippers, serial killers. Admittedly not the typical mother one met at Garden Club teas. But interesting.

"Dad said there was something you wanted to tell me," I continued.

"It's related in a way. Me being a reporter. No one ever kept secrets from me, so I'm not going to keep them from you. It's about your origins."

I felt ill at ease, and a little scared. After all these years I was filled with the same emotions that I had felt as a child. I had never asked about my life before adoption because I didn't want answers. Did I really want to know now? I let her proceed. She wanted me to know. That's why I was summoned.

"I've never asked you about the adoption."

Mother looked up and smiled.

"In those days people who adopted children weren't supposed to know anything about the birth parents or the life of the child prior to the adoption. Well, you know me. As an old Hearst reporter, I found out all there was to know."

She lowered her eyes. Sitting by a flowerbed, talking to the pile of tulip bulbs, she told me my story.

"You were born in Norwalk, Connecticut in 1949 as James Campbell. Your birth mother was the youngest of six children. Her mother had died giving birth to her. Her father was a seaman. He was in no position to raise the children. Relatives took the children in. All except for your mother. No one wanted another girl."

I knew I was an unwanted child but I never thought about the situation my birth mother might have been in. Unwanted as well. What a hell of a world.

"… Was a ward of the State," I returned to paying attention to my mother's narrative, "brought up in institutions. She became pregnant with you when she was sixteen. Your father would not or could not accept responsibility for you or her. He took off."

My mother looked up from the bulbs and into my face.

"Despite everything, she did want to keep you. She nursed you for six months."

She must have seen the bitterness in my eyes and felt the need to defend my birth mother.

"Then what happened?"

Mother reached for her trowel and picked at the earth, as if the answer to my question was buried under that soil.

"The State took you away from her and placed you in a foster home."

"Just because she was young?"

"There were problems."

"Like what?"

Did I really want to know?

"She was impatient with you. When you didn't respond the way she wanted, she hit you."

"Shit."

I knew there was something. Some reason why I hated this birth mother of mine. You can't hate your own mother. It's not natural. Not right. But I did.

"Don't judge her too hard," Mother said. She had read my face again. Once a reporter, always a reporter. "She was young. She had been dumped by her own family."

I changed the subject.

"Tell me about the foster parents."

"You really lucked out when it came to your foster mother. She loved you and wanted to adopt you as they had with two other foster children. But she couldn't afford to. Her husband had only a meager income. He worked in a gas station."

What would my life been like if my foster mother had adopted me? Maybe I'd be less of a loner. Could be running a successful garage in Connecticut. But I liked my current existence, the boat, the shamus business, books, baroque music, Oakland, Lori, even Monty.

"Your young life," Mother continued, "was a stormy one, disrupted frequently by your biological mother. She kept pestering the foster mother to let her take you home. Even though it was against the rules, your foster mother would relent. Your biological mother disciplined you harshly. When she thought you weren't walking soon enough, she spanked you. Crying hysterically, you would return to your foster mother. Finally the State authorities intervened and put a stop to the visits."

She dropped the trowel and, with a wrinkled blue-veined hand, patted down the soil she had stirred up.

"That was the way your life was until we adopted you."

"How old was I?"

"Three."

My mother's narrative affected me deeply. A wall, very much like the fence that enclosed my mother's vegetable garden, had existed between my adoptive parents and me as far back as my memory reached. It was now a little less high. I felt a different kind of distance. It was an interesting, moving account of this young boy, James Campbell. It was like listening to a story about someone else. Bullshit. James Campbell was Jim Wolf. It was me, me.

I stared down at my mother, her face turned upwards, blue eyes focused beyond me, her mind searching back over forty years. Her gray hair was held in place on her head by bobby pins. Strands that she had missed flayed out in all directions, hair that had once been a rich blond color. She was a beautiful woman in her youth, tall and strong. Decades of sun worship etched her face with wrinkles, yet a sculptor would still appreciate her contours.

Despite myself, I ploughed on, "What was my birth mother's name?"

"Thinking of looking her up? I wish you luck. Janice Sutcliff. Campbell was the father's name. Don't think you'll find her anymore in Norwalk. But that won't stop you. You're like me."

"No, I don't think I want to look her up."

Rage surged within me again.

"You will. You could never tolerate unsolved mysteries."

"The foster parents?"

"I believe they're still in Norwalk. I remember seeing the gas station. Dropped in and we chatted. He asked about you. The wife died of breast cancer some years back. Tanzi. Eugene Tanzi. On Route 7."

"Italian?"

"Yes."

"Interesting."

"Why?"

I told Mother about Lori. I had never confided about my personal life with either of my parents before that day. It felt good finally to be talking to her.

"Why don't you marry her?"

"Can't explain it."

"You had three mothers during your first three years of life. No wonder you don't attach to women that well."

"You're my mother," I blurted out.

She smiled up at me, accepting the statement.

"Could you help me with these roots?"

"Of course."

I walked down the hill and brought back a bucket for the tulips. I helped my mother get up and walk down the slope of the back lawn. She clung to my arm a little more than she needed to steady herself. I felt her warmth.

My thoughts turned from my mother to Susan. Was she adopted like me. Had she more than one mother? More than one father? What was her secret? I felt she must have one, linked to that photo. Did her hidden past return to kill her?

The morphine began to wear off and my dreamy state with it. Replaced by total confusion. My instincts and my own personal history led me in one direction. The photo. Susan's early life. Yet, that phone call to Susan setting up a deadly meeting led in another direction. Her husband Henry's two children. Nina warned me to go only by the facts. But the photo was a fact. The phone call was a fact. Conflicting facts. Conflicting directions.

A jolt brought me painfully back to my own immediate challenge. Surviving this ambulance ride.

"Could you just tell the driver to try to miss a crater every now and then?" I asked.

"We'll have you at Highland Hospital in a couple of minutes."

Highland? Shit. If I could have moved – they had me strapped in – I would have been out the back and taking my chances leaping into the traffic. Really unfair as Highland was the best facility for gunshot wounds. They've had so much practice. It's just that the damned place was a war zone.

I was about to suggest to the driver to slow down – I was in no hurry to get there – when the van came to a stop on its own, then backed up. Must be Highland. The driver opened the back doors and an Indian fellow, with a stethoscope around his neck, hopped into the van. He looked me over superficially, then turned away. He winked at the paramedic, gave her thumbs up, and hopped back out of the van. I must have been a disappointment. The only way I could have gotten some attention from that doctor would have been if my head had been chopped off and I held it in my hands.

No Time To Mourn

9.

The triage nurse at Highland gave me a cursory check, cleaned up my wound, and decided I would probably live. That gave me very low priority. She nodded her head at an attendant. He rolled me into a hallway jammed with more serious cases.

Five figures in white gowns gathered around the gurney in front of me. A stick of a young man lay on the middle of the bed looking like a lone toothpick in an ashtray. Thin bare arms covered with black and blue and needle marks. They started pounding on his chest. Then came the cart with the electrodes. Bam, bam, the body jerked with each surge of electricity. Barely a flicker on the heart monitor. Finally they pulled the sheet over his head and wheeled him away. Another death by drug overdose. Wouldn't even make the paper. Instinctively, I gripped my sheet. I was determined they were not going to throw some damned white cloth over my face.

A gurney holding an old drunk rolled into the place left vacant by the drug overdose. He reeked of drink and excrement. Great combination. He moaned and waved his hands, hitting at imaginary insects.

A crew flew by me pushing a gurney containing a pregnant teenager. Couldn't be more than fifteen. She was crying like the little child she still was. Her immense stomach moved in spasms, like the dome of a volcano preparing to erupt. She was minutes away from giving birth. No one with her, no boyfriend, not even her mother. Like I said, combat duty, unsung heroes fighting a losing battle in a world we all deny existed.

I lay there for what seemed like hours, hoping Lori would show up. People kept streaming in: a shooting victim whose entire chest was covered in blood, a wretching drunk, a heroin addict screaming from withdrawal agony, a stabbing victim with the knife still in place in her shoulder, a homeless man complaining of a strange pain in the chest, hoping to get a bed for the night.

The whole scene humbled me. To be grazed by a bullet and have a rib or two broken had no more significance than a splinter in the finger. Far more important battles with life and death consequences went on in that hallway. Maybe I deserved their neglect.

I decided I had witnessed enough. I planned to get up off that gurney, walk out of that mad house, call a cab, and go home to Monty. Pushing myself up, I got woozy, and fell back again onto the thin gurney mattress. Something was definitely wrong. I couldn't make it.

That's when Lori walked into the hallway. She had washed her face and reapplied her makeup. There was a glow all around her that created a halo effect. Damned woman looked like an angel descended directly from Heaven to rescue me. The fact that she was standing between me and the light fixture in the ceiling might have had something to do with it. It affected everyone in the crowded hallway. The place became quiet. Even my drunken companion stopped moaning and stared at her.

"You look like shit. They left you lying here all this time? If this were 'ER' there'd be six doctors hovering over you. It's 4 A.M., for Christ's sake."

"This is real life, not TV. It doesn't get much more real than this."

No Time To Mourn

"I got to get you some help."

"First, tell me what happened? Did Nina grill you?"

"She turned me over to the nicest detective. Ed Karpaki or something. But this guy, Ollie, kept butting in."

"That's Richard Oliphant. White guy? Close cropped hair always perfectly combed, very formal?"

"That's him."

"Nina's partner. He's a pain."

"Nina and Ollie. I remember Kukla, Fran and Ollie."

"You would. Didn't he ask you about Susan?"

"Oh, that. Don't worry," Lori patted her purse, "you can count on me. Nothing said about what's in here. I was a little fuzzy about everything. I stressed the state of shock I was in. Ed was very understanding."

"Was Nina as understanding?" I asked.

The drunk was back to moaning and swatting non-existent flies. Two orderlies rolled in another gurney. This one held a black guy with a bloody bandage wrapped around his head. Lori was oblivious to everything around us.

"All business, that Nina. She was running the show. You should see the way those men hopped to it when she said anything. A pleasure to watch. She was busy getting all the crime scene people doing what she wanted them to do, fingerprints, photos. Really impressive. I loved every minute. Then Nina came over to me. She mentioned you."

"What did she want?"

"Said she had some questions for you when you recover. I don't think she's too happy about you being mixed up in this."

"Great."

Lori looked down at the wound on my shoulder and shook her head.

"They check you out?"

"Not really."

"I'll get you a doctor and out of here in no time. You got coverage, right?"

"Sort of."

"Sort of? You either got it or you ain't."

"Blue Cross."

"Where's the 'sort of' come in?"

"High deductible."

Add that to a list of the negatives of being a private eye. We've got to insure ourselves. That can be costly these days.

"Too damn bad. I'm not leaving you in this slaughterhouse even if I've got to pay for it."

"Lori…"

She ignored me, turned, and ploughed right through a door marked "Hospital Employees Only." She was back in a minute flat towing a young doctor behind her. Literally. She was holding his hand and dragging the chap. Short blond hair, fashionable tiny tinted oval glasses, white coat, regulation stethoscope around his neck. He had a sheepish grin on his face. I'd swear he was blushing. The poking began in earnest.

"How is he, Doctor Ellison?" Lori looked up into his face as if he were Marcus Welby himself.

"The gunshot wound doesn't look serious. I'll have to report it. But he may have a broken rib." He turned away from her and addressed me. "Miss Mazzetti says you fainted."

Miss Mazzetti? It had been a while since I'd heard her referred to that formally.

"Yes, twice, and I get a bit dizzy when I sit up."

"You probably have a concussion. But it could be more serious. I would recommend an MRI. Miss Mazzetti wants you released to Summit. I can arrange that."

"Call me Lori, Doctor. I told you that." Her deep blue eyes were open wide, absorbing the poor sucker. He'd give her anything she wanted, even a quart or two of morphine.

"Lori then. You can call me Eric." He smiled.

She was good to her word. I was out of that snake pit in half an hour.

No Time To Mourn

Summit gave me an X-ray. My ribs were bruised not broken. Then they taped me up and ran me through the MRI machine. I know it's impossible, but I swear I could feel the magnetic waves going through my body. The radiologist tentatively concluded all I had was a minor concussion. Promised to let me know if anything else turned up. He told me I could go home. I was to take two eight-hundred milligram Motrins every four hours. Not very impressive medicine. I was warned not to drive and asked to report any recurring dizzy spells.

I had no intention of following the doc's instructions about not driving. I needed to take a cab from the hospital to Susan's house to pick up my car. Figured I'd kill two birds with one stone. I called Lori and got the name of the cab driver who had dropped off Susan on her last night. Al Swineheart. Yellow Cabs located him. A half hour later the cab pulled up in front of Summit. An odd-looking fellow jumped out. Tall, narrow on top, wide at the bottom. Bedraggled long gray hair hung down from the sides of his dome-like bald head. His yellowed teeth twisted in an unnatural way as they tried to fit into a jaw to narrow for them. Looked a bit like Big Bird gone to seed. No way would I have trusted Swineheart with my wad of dough.

"Where to?" he asked.

"Where'd you take Susan Henry Friday night?"

"Where I always take her. You a cop?"

"Private. Name's Wolf."

"Cool," he said, wincing into something I think he thought was a wink.

He opened the door for me and I climbed in. He had the Oldies radio station tuned in just a bit too loud. I sat back and let him drive. I decided to tackle him when we got to the scene of the crime. He had other ideas. The talkative type.

"I liked the lady," he said as he turned down the radio, "but, boy, could she drink."

"Tell me what happened?"

"Already told the cops."

"She hired me to protect her. I'm damned if I'm going to let her murderer get away with it. So tell me, too."

"Same, same. I picked her up on schedule. Been drinking more than usual, and that was a hell of a lot. Kept muttering something about a holster. Weird. Mentioned your name a couple of times. 'Tell Wolf,' she said. Then she would mutter that holster thing again."

"I heard the same when I left her at Big Emma's. Then what?"

"The fog was so goddamn thick I had trouble findin' the place. And I go up there most every night. For some reason she liked me. Always asked Yellow for Big Bird. That's what everybody calls me. You figure it. I was smoking a joint when the call came in, so I was kind of spaced out. This tune was runnin' through my head that night, 'House of the Rising Sun.' Spooky. Made it to her place somehow. Tried to walk her to her door. No way. So I just picked her up and carried her in."

"I saw you."

"I get it, super sleuth. Didn't see you. Course in that fog I wouldn't have seen a yellow submarine struttin' up the street." He laughed, like it was a joke. I wondered if the guy was ever not stoned.

We were winding up Mandana and had entered the Crocker-Highlands neighborhood. The fog had begun to clear. The area looked positively pleasant. Swineheart slowed down as we approached Susan's house. Yellow tape blocked off the property. A white Crime Scene van was still out front. My car was parked by the curb behind the van. At least no ticket.

"Hey, look at the place," Al said. "Far freakin' out. Just like 'Homicide.'"

I wondered if he ever bent Lori's ear talking about TV shows. He stopped just behind my car.

"So what happened once you got inside?"

No Time To Mourn

"I took her into her bedroom, like I always do when she's in that condition. Plopped her down on the bed."

"Take your fare from her purse?"

"No way, man. I never touch her purse. Joe pays me up front at the bar."

"So you left?"

"Not right away."

"Why not?"

"She woke up and tried to get off the bed. Kept saying 'pointment.' Something like that. I finally figured it out. She was expecting someone. So I helped her up and half-walked, half-carried her into her study. Sat her at that big desk of hers. She plopped her head down and fell asleep."

"Then you looked in her purse."

"Cut that shit out. The cops tried the same thing on me. I've had a hundred opportunities to take money from her. Never did. Never would. Not that I haven't been tempted. If I had, you wouldn't see me around here. I'd be in Mexico."

At least I knew now how Susan ended up sitting at her desk in her study. Swineheart confirmed Joe's report that Susan had an appointment with someone at the house. Yes, she was set up. Edith was the most likely person to have set her up. But then why turn up and implicate herself? Maybe the brother, Edward. I had questions for both of them.

"That's all?"

"Yeah, I walked out."

"And forgot to lock the door."

"Like I said, I was spaced out. There's ten bucks on the meter. I got to get back to work."

"Wouldn't think of keeping you from it."

I gave him twenty bucks and he took off with a smile on his face. Did I believe him about the money? Bet he peeled off a bill or two here and there. But did it matter? He certainly didn't shoot the woman or hire Red. At least I knew how Susan ended up in her study. And that holster stuff. Important. Something she was holding back from me. But what did it mean?

10.

The look on Nina's face as I walked into the homicide detectives' office of the Oakland Police Department was not encouraging. Not a scowl. More an all-business solemnity. She avoided eye contact.

A dozen desks were scattered haphazardly around the large room. Each one had a computer monitor and competed with its neighbor as to how much paperwork could be piled on top of it. No extra chairs sat next to any of the desks. Interrogations evidently took place elsewhere.

Nina rose as I entered. She was dressed in a brown knee-length skirt, a matching tailored jacket, and a white blouse. Richard Oliphant, her partner, sat stiffly in his chair at the other end of the room, glaring at me.

"This way," Ollie muttered gruffly, as he stood up.

He gestured toward one of two small doors at the rear of the room. Nina strode over with me to join him. He opened the door revealing a tiny room, with barely the space for a small wooden table and three chairs. The room was painted a sickly dirty light yellow, the desk and chairs a pale green. No Martha Stewart décor for Oakland PD. I noticed someone had carved the initials "C. R." in the molding around the door. Made you wonder. How C. R. got the knife into the room and why was

No Time To Mourn

he left alone long enough to make his mark on the place's history?

Ollie waited until I had entered and then moved to close the door. Nina was already comfortably seated at the table. The room pressed in on me, claustrophobic, cold, bureaucratic. I wanted to confess immediately so that they would lead me to a spacious cell where I could breathe. But I wasn't the guy who had killed Susan. I took the chair offered me opposite the two. Ollie seated himself and placed the tape recorder in the middle of the table.

"Do you mind if we tape this interview?" Ollie asked.

He wore a bow tie, red spanners, and a clean pressed white dress shirt. No doubt he thought the outfit made him look like a professional police detective. Seemed more like a small town insurance agent attending a Rotary luncheon.

"No."

"You are here voluntarily and may leave at any time. You have a right to have your lawyer present. We are conducting a homicide investigation into the murder of Susan Henry. We have reason to believe you will be able to furnish us information concerning Mrs. Henry and the events leading up to her death. Do you understand this?"

Ollie loved these formalities. The more he pontificated, the less I was inclined to be forthcoming.

"Yes."

"Please, speaking into the microphone, give us your name, occupation, and place of residence."

I obliged.

"Now, Wolf," Nina proceeded.

I appreciated her not calling me Jimmie. With straight, black, shoulder-length hair, silky light brown complexion, and full red lips, she hardly looked like a mother of two, and certainly not a homicide detective. More like an anchorwoman for the six o'clock news.

"Please tell us in your own words everything that occurred last Friday afternoon and evening. Take your time and leave nothing out. Begin with how you met Mrs. Henry and your conversation with her at Big Emma's."

I gave them as full an account as I could, leaving out only the photo business. Nina wrote a word down every now and then on the blank sheet of paper in front of her. Ollie scribbled away as if he didn't trust the tape recorder, covering a dozen pages in a legal-sized lined yellow pad. I went on for about forty-five minutes. When I concluded, Nina resumed the interrogation.

"Just a few more questions. When you went outside Big Emma's and walked past the man sitting in the red Saab…"

"I believe you call him 'Red,'" Ollie said. "Was that his real name?"

"Don't know his real name. That's what Susan called him."

"So she knew him?" Nina asked.

"Of course not. She made up the name because of his red car. And his face did appear to be reddish."

"For identification purposes only we will refer to the gentleman you spotted in that car as 'Red.'" Ollie was having fun.

"When you walked past Red, sitting in the Saab, how far away were you?" Nina resumed her interrogation.

"About two feet."

"Was he facing your way?"

"No, he was reading a newspaper."

"So you only got a side view of him. It was foggy?"

"Yes, but he had his dome light on."

"When he ran his car up on the sidewalk in front of Big Emma's you saw him again?"

"Not too clearly. I was blinded by the headlights."

"Later that evening, when you chased him up the gangway, you saw him for a third time."

I nodded.

"How far away was he?"

"Ten feet."

No Time To Mourn

"Fog again?"

"Yes, but I was just about on top of him."

"Could you pick this man out of a lineup?" Ollie asked.

"Yes. Pretty sure."

I felt foolish. I'm a private eye and pride myself in my ability to make cross-examination proof identifications. Everything happened so fast. It was dark. Fog. Humbled me. I understood better Susan's difficulty identifying Red.

"You're a great help," he muttered. "I assume then that you were prepared to shoot this man. That's murder, you know."

"Self-defense, buddy. Red shot me. I don't like getting shot. I take it personally and fire back. Simple as that. If I'd hit the bastard, Susan would be alive now."

"You said you aimed at his back. A jury might not think it was that simple."

I pushed my cup away and stared at Ollie. He averted his eyes. The guy was on my case. However, I understood the tough questioning on identifying Red. Nina and Ollie were convinced, for reasons they didn't divulge, that he was the killer. They were determined to extract testimony that would hold up in a court of law.

"If you don't mind, there's something I want to say."

I leaned forward in my chair.

"We're doing the questioning, Wolf," Ollie said.

"Try listening for a change. It's not just you two who now know I can identify Red. He knows as well. With Susan dead, I'm the only one who can tie him to her murder. It's in his interest to kill me. We don't know where he is but he knows where I live. What are you going to do about it?"

"Nothing," Ollie said.

He growled the word, sticking his chin forward like he was trying out for the role of Mussolini. I turned to Nina. She looked down at her lap.

"Thanks," I said, and started to get up.

"Just a minute," Nina spoke softly, "we'd like you to bring your gun in tomorrow so we can test fire it. This is voluntary, of course, but we could get a court order if necessary. At the same time we need to take your fingerprints and a blood sample."

"Happy to oblige." Nina was my friend but what was she after? "You don't think I shot her?"

"You have told us that you shot at the red Saab and believe you hit it. If we can find that car, your bullet may still be lodged in it. We need your fingerprints as part of an elimination process. And you appeared to have dripped quite a bit of blood throughout the house."

"Sorry for dirtying the floor."

"You are not being charged with anything at this time," Ollie said.

Ollie placed his emphasis on the last three words. He wore what he no doubt thought was his fiercest face. With that bow tie he looked more like a five-year-old boy protesting being dragged to church than a threatening cop. I rose from my chair and started to walk out of the room.

"One moment, Mr. Wolf," Ollie said and started paging through his notes. "Please sit down."

I dropped back into my chair.

"There is one little matter that confuses me," he continued. "That first telephone call to Detective Peterson. Am I correct in assuming you were asking her to give you confidential police information?"

Nina stiffened and gave her partner a murderous side glance.

"Are you referring to the license number business?"

"Yes."

"I had a client that I had reason to believe was being stalked by our friend Red. That's against the law in this state. More importantly, I felt, rightly it appears, that she was in danger. It seemed proper to me to report the license number to the police. Since I knew Detective Peterson as a very conscientious police officer, and I was afraid to wait until morning, I called her at her home. I simply gave her the information in my possession."

"You didn't ask her for anything?"

"I asked her to have the department look into this matter."

"She called you back?"

"Certainly. She had taken my call seriously enough to check out the license number. The result of that check worried her sufficiently to call me to be sure I was all right. I told her about the shooting at the dock and she promised to have patrolmen keep an eye on my boat as well as Susan's house."

"Anything further, Detective Oliphant?" Nina asked acidly. Her dark eyes focused on him. There was a frown on her face.

"A couple more questions, if you don't mind." Ollie had a look on his face that suggested he didn't give a shit who minded.

"Go ahead," I said, turning toward Ollie and sporting my most humble expression.

"You said you looked into Mrs. Henry's purse."

"Yes, I did."

"Why?"

"I was looking for a large wad of hundred dollar bills. Remember, I told you earlier about that money when I described the scene with her at Big Emma's."

"How much do you figure was in the purse?"

"I don't know. Could be ten thousand dollars or more."

"Did you find the money?"

"No."

"Would you mind, Mr. Wolf," Ollie asked, "if we made a search of your boat? We would also appreciate it if you gave us access to your bank accounts."

He had a smug smile on his face. I knew he was asking only to irritate me. He was succeeding.

"Damn right I would mind. If you're suggesting I stole from Susan, you had better get a goddamn search warrant."

I began to rise from the table.

"We're not accusing you of anything," Ollie continued. "We are only going by your testimony that there was ten thousand dollars or so in that purse earlier that day, that you looked inside the purse after Mrs. Henry's death, and it was empty. Everyone who had access to the contents of that purse is of interest to us."

"Go check on that cab driver Swineheart, or the daughter, Edith." I stood towering over the bastard. "Do you think I would be stupid enough to tell you about the empty purse if I had stolen the money?"

I headed for the door. Ollie jumped up and placed himself between the exit and me.

"There is one more matter I want to make perfectly clear," he said. "This is a murder investigation. We have had problems with you in the past. I will not tolerate your interference on this case. It's against the law for private investigators to involve themselves in homicide cases. I will insist that the law be enforced if you so much as even tiptoe near this one."

He spat out the words "private investigators." What a bastard. Let him try to earn a living as a PI. He was lucky he was on the city payroll.

"Be real, Oliphant."

I push roughly past him and headed out the door. I turned my head and saw him start to charge out after me. Nina placed her hand on his arm to restrain him. I had both a killer and a bone-headed cop after me. What did he expect me to do? Sit on the deck of my boat with a target pinned to my chest?

No Time To Mourn

11.

I lowered myself through the hatchway into *Sea Wolf's* cabin. It was five o'clock and still light outside. The fog had lifted sufficiently so that I could make out the Alameda shoreline. Comforting. My world had been restored. For the moment, in any event. My shoulder ached a bit, but it was my ribs that gave the most trouble. They sure as hell felt like they were fractured.

Monty, wide awake, stretched out in her glass tank. She took me in with those bullet-like black eyes of hers. I reached into her tank and picked her up. Carefully, very carefully. She needed some handling. I hung her carefully around my shoulders to remind her of her dancing days with Sheila. Had to keep her away from my sensitive ribs. Her warm body tightened gently around my arms. Only a slight constriction. Kind of erotic. I could see where Sheila was coming from.

She snuggled in closer around my arms. Was that damned animal constricting for real? Enough togetherness. I never was much good at relationships, even with a damned snake. I unwrapped Monty and placed her back into her tank. Time to feed her. It is not recommended to leave a seven-foot python hungry for long. They've been known to get confused and mistake their owners for dinner.

Tim Wohlforth

She only ate once a week. Finicky like most pythons in captivity. Insisted on eating whole mice and rats. She had to be handfed. The trick was to hand-feed her – without feeding her your hand. I'd gotten her accustomed to freshly killed mice I bought from a pet store. Kept them frozen.

Monty's beady eyes followed my every move. I opened the refrigerator and then the freezer door. Her head was up and her tongue shot out in an erratic searching pattern. She knew what goodies lay behind that door. Monty's half of the freezer was stuffed with frozen white mice. Mine held Trader Joe's enchiladas and tamales. Skim milk for my granola, low fat milk to make lattés, fresh squeezed orange juice, a couple of bottles of Anchor Steam filled the bottom of the refrigerator. I'm not much for elaborate cooking on a boat.

I placed a stiff, but rather plump, mouse on top of the fridge to thaw out. No Ben & Jerry's for Monty. She was cold blooded enough as it was.

I curled up on the dinette bench while Monty's dinner thawed. My mind finally cleared enough to think about Susan's death. I knew, and I was convinced from my interrogation that Nina and Ollie also knew, that Red shot Susan. If Edith was Red's employer, then she must have made the phone call to set up an appointment with her. But why turn up just before Red arrived? Stupid to expose herself. If Edith didn't make the phone call, my best guess was Edward, the son. In that case, maybe Edward also called Edith precisely to set her up as a prime murder suspect. With Edith also out of the way he wouldn't have to split his inheritance. Yes, Edward fitted. But I had to meet the children, take their measures, ask them both some questions.

Then there was the photo business. Didn't fit with the Edward and Edith scenario. Susan didn't believe for a minute that Edith or Junior could possibly hire someone to kill her. And she knew them better than I did. Susan insisted the photo was important. I had to know more about that picture and about her mother. Lori still had my manila envelope. I would have to pick it up from her as soon as possible. I knew just the people to analyze it.

Could there be some connection between the photo and the two Henry children? I couldn't conceive of one. It's one thing to have two tracks to investigate. It is quite another when these tracks lead in opposite and unconnected directions. Confusing. I needed to know more.

Monty stared at me.

"Don't worry, Honey. I didn't forget your snack."

I took a pair of tweezers from a holder attached to her tank. I picked up the now limp mouse and lowered the creature into her tank. Then I tapped the glass. Zap. Monty struck and down went mousy. Soon the mouse was no more than a bump along Monty's otherwise sleek physique.

Used to gross me out. But no more. I've thought it through. One long food chain beginning with bacteria. Once you get higher up, you come to the predators. Monty's well up there but we're the highest. That's why she's the one in a tank.

I put a CD of Christopher Parkening playing classical guitar in the player and prepared to get some rest. I poured myself a short Oban neat, chugged down two Motrins, and climbed into my berth.

"Jimmie, thanks for the way you handled that license search in the interview." Nina was on the phone. She had awakened me.

"Look, you were just trying to help me out. The least I could do."

"Ollie's going to be on my case from now on. Not to mention on yours. You didn't win any brownie points with him today. He's serious about nailing you if he can. There's a couple of things I've got to tell you for your own safety. So listen up, man."

"You mean I was right about Red."

"Yes. We retrieved the bullet from the hull of your boat."

"Damn it. I forgot to check for the bullet hole. Hope you didn't gouge out the side. You have no idea what a hassle it'll be to fix it."

"You got bigger worries. Hear me out. The bullet we dug out of the side of your boat matches perfectly one found in the wall behind Susan. She had been shot at point blank range. The bullet passed right through her skull. By the angle of the trajectory she must have been sitting up staring at her attacker. Twenty-two caliber. Our forensic people believe it was fired from a semiautomatic chambered for subsonic ammunition. Probably a Ruger Mark II."

"I'm not up on this subsonic stuff."

"You take a semiautomatic and fit it with a small caliber chamber designed to fire a bullet that travels slower than the speed of sound. Then you add a silencer. There are marks on the bullets that suggest a silencer was used. The result is a weapon that sounds no louder than the ping you heard. It's not your run of the mill street weapon."

"I'm beginning to get the picture."

"It's a professional assassin's gun, designed to be fired at short range where it would be fatal. Almost silent. Tells us something about this Red motherfucker, doesn't it?"

"That he was paid to bump off Susan."

"More than that. There is a weird upside to this. He has a weapon that is neither that accurate nor usually fatal at distances beyond twenty feet. When he gets around to trying his hand at your assassination, he will figure out a way to catch you unawares and up-close."

"Comforting, but I see what you mean. His attempt to run me down was an impulse thing. Then I caught him when he was trying to sneak up on the boat and set up a professional-type hit. When we faced each other down, the guy ran for it."

I involuntarily looked around the boat's cabin. Like the fellow was hiding somewhere close.

No Time To Mourn

"One more thing. I had 'em do a match with the bullet that killed the husband. Perfect."

"I thought he was shot from a distance."

"Not really. Red parked his car and stepped out right in front of them and bang, or I should say ping. Probably not more than ten feet away when he fired. By the way, we found the license plate Red's been using. I'm sure he's stolen a replacement by now."

"Where?"

"Behind the dumpster by Big Emma's."

"Guy's got a sense of humor."

"He's taunting us. That's why he runs around in a red Saab. It's an ego trip."

"Anything else I should know?"

"We've arrested Edith."

"Why?"

"The money. While you were lying around that hospital, we've been busy. Had a tail on both Edith and Edward. Saturday afternoon she pulled her cycle up in front of a padlocked bar on Martin Luther King Jr. Used to be a blues club."

"I know the joint. The elevated BART line runs right past it."

I could visualize the place. A real eyesore, chain on the door, barred windows with broken glass, weeds grown up around it.

"You got it. She met a large black dude. He unlocked the door and the two went inside. They both stayed in there about fifteen minutes. When they left, they split up. Our guys phoned in, and I had them bring in the dude. He has a record so he was cooperative. Owns the property. Edith had given him $10,000 in cash as a deposit. Told him she wanted to open a dyke bar."

Made some sense. Spruced up and with a bevy of large ladies to protect it, might work. At least the mystery of the missing wad of dough was solved.

"So you got her for theft?"

"It's sewed up. Both her prints and Susan's are on the loot."

"Ollie knew this when he was grilling me this afternoon?"

"Yes."

"The guy's a scum bag."

"You- "

A roar partially obliterated Nina's voice.

"Speak up. A boat's passing."

"You're making me seasick. Just as well you didn't hear what I said. He figures Edith for the murder."

"But Red shot Susan."

The boat's swell began rocking the *Sea Wolf*.

"He thinks she hired him. She makes one last effort to get money out of Susan. When she doesn't cough up, she grabs the cash out of her purse, runs out the door, and calls in Red to finish her off."

"I don't buy it. The Henry estate is worth millions. Why petty theft?"

"Good question."

"Either way you've got to find Red before he kills me. Right? Got any ideas on how to do that?"

"That's why I'm calling you. Since Ollie thinks Edith hired the guy, he's talked the DA into letting her out on low bail tomorrow morning. Then he's having her watched day and night. Also Edward. He thinks it's possible the two were working together on it. They're the ones with a five mil motive. It's not the way I wanted to go about it."

"What was your idea?"

"Put the manpower on you. Red will most likely return to wipe out his only witness. Then we bag him. But I got voted down."

"Great. Ollie's not the one to pay the price if he guesses wrong."

"You be careful, man. This Red's a bad one, and I'm not talkin' in Ebonics."

No Time To Mourn

After Nina's phone call, I tried to sleep. No way. I lay on my bunk and closed my eyes. Then I opened them and glanced up at the porthole. Was that a human shape out there? Red's face? The long barrel of his narrow gun? Or just a puff of fog? I tensed my body and listened for the ping. Nothing. Damn it. To hell with him.

I decided to walk over to Big Emma's and retrieve the photo. That way I could get work started on it in the morning. Any excuse to see Lori. Hadn't seen her since our time together early Saturday morning at Highland Hospital.

I crept along the slightly swaying dock, trying my best to stay in its center. The fog had rolled back in. More dense than Friday night. I had no flashlight. Useless in this kind of fog. And no gun. Why carry a gun for a quick walk to Big Emma's, I reasoned. I figured Red would go back to his lair to regroup before stalking me again. He would want things to cool down following Susan's murder. That's how he had reacted after he shot Edward Henry. But now, out in the fog once more, the fog that had hidden Red in the past, I wasn't so sure I had made the smartest decision. I felt as I had felt the night he tried to run me over in front of Big Emma's. As I had felt the moments before he shot at me when I chased him down this very dock.

My foot caught on a coiled rope. Damn. Nearly tripped. The gangway to the shore rose out of the mist. Thankfully, I grabbed hold of the rope railing and climbed up onto dry – actually quite damp – land.

It was almost nine o'clock and Jack London Square was deathly quiet. The damned foghorn bleated away every ninety seconds. A shiver went down my spine. I sensed something malevolent out there in the fog, just beyond my vision. I was beginning to wonder if this trip was such a hot idea. I was vulnerable on the boat but now I was even an easier target. Then I shrugged my shoulders. I had vowed not to live in fear. I'd take my chances.

I quickened my pace once I reached the sidewalk along the waterfront. Keeping just a few inches from the railing, I made my way toward Big Emma's. I stopped. Something, damn it, something was out there. I strained to hear. No footsteps behind me.

The railing disappeared. Some massive structure. I remembered the Pavilion, a large permanent canvas tent used for weddings and other private parties. No action that night. Completely dark. I saw a huge dark shape undulating in the fog. Trying to reach me, smother me. I stopped.

A puff of wind. The fog cleared for a second. The black behemoth proved to be the Pavilion's canvas billowing in the light wind. Like some gargantuan kite that had fallen from the sky and gotten wedged along the embankment. It created rippling shadows in the fogbank. I stood still and watched for a minute, fascinated by the billowing cloth. So lifelike yet so harmless. Damn it, my nerves were completely shot.

The wind died down and the fog closed in on me again. I heard a slight noise. A rat? No. More like breathing. I sensed eyes bearing down upon me. I had been right, Goddamn it. Something was out there in the fog.

I turned to face the parking lot, or what must have been the parking lot, for the fog blinded me completely. I searched the darkness. There. I began to see something. A rough line of dark giant shapes that didn't belong. A deafening roar blasted my eardrums. A wall of bright lights rushed toward me.

12.

My first thought was Red and his goddamned Saab. But there were too many headlights for a car. And the noise. Shit, bikes. They must have been sitting with their engines off waiting for me.

I ran toward Big Emma's. Roaring engines plunged at me out of the fog. I turned and tried to sprint back to the *Sea Wolf*. More gargantuan bikes. Blinding lights surrounded me. I couldn't escape. I stopped, pressing my hands to my ears to block out the sound. Someone was shouting at me. I heard "Wolf." Nothing else intelligible. Then I saw the outline of a massive figure approaching me, holding a beer bottle with the end broken off.

"Turn off those Goddamn engines," I shouted. "I can't hear you. And the lights. You're blinding me. What do you want?"

The leader made a gesture and the noise and light abated. It was only then that I was able to make out the figure of a very large woman. She was wearing a World War II Nazi helmet, a leather vest but no shirt, leather pants and boots. A black stiletto dripping red blood was tattooed on her enormous bicep. Ten other massive ladies, dressed similarly, sat on the Harleys that encircled me. Several of them were smoking. Camels, I assumed.

"Wolf, I'm going to cut you up, you bastard. It's because of you Edith's in jail."

"That's not true," I shouted back. "They had a make on her even before they interviewed me."

"You're the witness on that money being in Susan's purse Friday afternoon."

"Others knew that, too. Come on, you're not helping Edith. You're making things worse."

"You think I'm some stupid pussy? I'll cut your balls off."

The women surrounding us roared with laughter. Then something struck me about her. She was close enough so that I could see her face. There was fear in her eyes. I posed no physical threat to her. It must be her worry about Edith's fate. Maybe I could reach her.

"Edith's in deep shit. They may charge her with murder. I can help you get her out of it, if you give me a chance."

"Fuck."

"You've got to let me help her."

"I don't trust you, dickhead."

"You don't need to trust me. Why don't we all go over to Big Emma's? I'll buy you a beer. We can talk things out. If you don't like what you hear, you've still got me."

"Better not try to fuck with us," the leader muttered. "You're riding on the back of my bike."

She pushed me along, prodding me with her broken bottle, toward her Harley. Swinging on top of the monster, she kick-started the bike. Her companions followed suit. The deafening noise and bright lights returned. I swung onto the seat behind her, grabbing the handles below the seat. A red-checkered bandanna protruded from her back pocket. Emblazoned on the back of her jacket was a large skull and crossbones with the words Devil's Dykes Motorcycle Club – Oakland Local.

We blasted off toward Big Emma's. Fog swirled around us, the Harley's headlights reflecting back upon us. How my captor saw where she was going I'm not too sure. It soon became apparent that she didn't see that clearly. We banged into a pothole so deep half the front wheel disappeared. I lurched forward, smacking into the lady's massive back. A stabbing pain penetrated my bruised rib cage. Involuntarily, I cried out. My Harley driver didn't even slow down.

A parked car sprung out of the fog right in front of us, like a skeleton in a fun house. The bike swerved at the last second. The car's fender brushed my knee. Another car, and another, and another. We were in the middle of the parking lot. The Harley wobbled precariously as she slowed down slightly, turned a sharp left, sped up, and barreled through a tiny space between two parked cars. I heard bellowing machines all around me. We tumbled out onto Broadway, the other bikes by our side. Horns honked, a red light flashed by the railroad tracks. The twelve of us, now in formation, banged across the tracks and thundered up the street, like Hitler's Blitzkrieg entering Poland.

"Slow down, for shit's sake," I yelled into the wind.

No answer. Then the screeching of many brakes. Eleven massive hulks of black iron bounced over the curb and slid to a stop within inches of the front door of Big Emma's. I had discovered Edith's driving instructors.

I will remember for the rest of my days the expression on Lori's face when I stumbled into her joint surrounded by my eleven female companions. It was as if a young woman had walked unannounced into her parents' home with an unmarried Kennedy hanging on her arm. Surprise mixed with sheer joy.

"Introduce me to your friends."

"Meet the Devil's Dykes Motorcycle Club."

"Fabulous."

Lori threw herself into the middle of the crowd, insisting on kissing each one of the ladies on the cheek. I'd swear some blushed. When I was able to get Lori's attention again, I had her seat the mob in the back while I steered the leader to the booth under the portrait of Big Emma. I looked up at my favorite mound of flesh. That night she faced some serious size competition.

"A round of drinks for everybody," I shouted.

Joe came out from behind the bar to serve them. Lori had settled in with the gang, her little blond head bobbing up and down as she talked away. I could see each gang member clearly now that they were in the light. Two blacks, three Hispanics, one Filipino, one Chinese, and the rest white. All wore identical leather vests with the club emblem on the back. To be honest, they were not all large. Three were pretty thin, and one was positively tiny. When sitting on those Harleys, motors blasting away, lights on me, they all appeared monstrous.

Joe brought a bottle of Wild Turkey to their table. Wasn't going to be a cheap night for me. At least I still had my balls.

I turned to my companion. I was happy to note she had dropped her broken bottle before entering Big Emma's. Her hair was black and cut very short, almost a crew cut. Her enormous breasts, unencumbered by a bra, threatened at any moment to fall out of her leather vest. The odor of too many cigarettes clung to her like fecal matter. Yet her large round face had a childlike character. As if she had grown bigger over the years, not necessarily older.

"Your name is?"

"Mildred."

"Mildred what?"

"Mildred. Now what's this about charging Edith with murder? I thought it was just that damned wad of dough."

"They haven't yet, but they're thinking about it. Got her a lawyer?"

"No."

"Let me give you a name. Sandra Jacobs. Very able defense lawyer. Call her tonight and mention me. She'll have her out in the morning. I've been informed the bail will be set low. You can raise some money?"

"Sure. We're standing by Edith. She did it for us. The money I mean. She wanted so bad to open a bar where we could all hang out and be ourselves. And it was her money really."

"Her money?"

"Well, she and Edward should have inherited the old man's dough. Instead he leaves it all to Susan in trust. Whenever she asked Susan for money, she'd refer her to Edward. He's the executor. He was no help, always lecturing Edith about her life style. Pompous bastard. That money and a lot more should be hers by right."

After Joe had taken care of the crew in the back, he came over to our table. Shouts and laughter came from the motorcycle gang. Lori had them enthralled. I ordered my usual Oban neat, while Mildred asked for a pint of Sierra Nevada and a double shot of Wild Turkey. Must be the club drink. Better than meth.

"I doubt if the law will see it that way. She'll probably have to cop a plea. If anybody can get Edith a good deal, it's Sandra. The money business is not my concern. I assume you believe she didn't murder Susan?"

"Of course not. Edith's a softy really. I got to watch out for her all the time. Protect her, you know what I mean."

Mildred roughly rubbed her eyes with her large hands, dirty with cycle grease. Black spots surrounded reddened eyelids.

"It's been one hell of a day," she continued.

Joe showed up with our drinks. She swallowed the whiskey in one gulp, washing it down with half the glass of beer. Then she wiped the foam off her mouth with the back of her hand. I noticed a tattooed red heart on her forearm with "Edith" in the center.

"I hope you're right about her. Look, you better call Sandra now. Tell her to arrange for Edith to meet me as soon as she springs her. I need to ask her some questions."

"You gonna help her or just grill her like the cops?"

Her eyes narrowed. She lifted her enormous arm, cradling her empty shot glass. Was she going to fling it into my face?

"I will give her a fair hearing. Anyway, the murder business is the cops' concern. I've been told to keep my nose out of it."

She waved the glass in Joe's direction in a beckoning gesture.

"So what is your concern?"

"Red."

"Red?"

"It's a long story, but the bottom line is there's a bastard out there trying to kill me. Maybe Edith can help me with Red, and I can help her in return. She ever mention a fat guy with a red face to you? Drives a red Saab."

"Never. Edith doesn't hang out with guys." She spit out the last word. "No hard feelings?"

"Of course not."

I didn't add how much I enjoyed the roaring bikes and her broken bottle. I wrote down the phone number of my lawyer Sandra Jacobs for her. Always kept it in my wallet for emergencies. Mildred headed for the pay-phone at the end of the bar.

I sat in my booth mulling over my interview with Mildred. I couldn't dismiss completely the thought that Edith was connected in some way to the murder of Susan. There was always the possibility Edith and Junior conspired together to get rid of Susan and inherit millions. I was not about to let Mildred know this as I needed Edith's cooperation.

What really pissed me was to have to pussyfoot around Susan's murder. Nina had made it abundantly clear that the cops were not going to protect me. I had to get Red. The only way I could do that was to try to find out who had hired him and then trace him through his boss. That meant find out who killed Susan. That arrogant asshole in spanners. Not his goddamn life that was on the line.

Fuck Ollie. First, I'd nail the bastard who was trying to kill me. I'd worry about Ollie later.

I got up, waved goodbye to Lori, and told Joe to put everything on my tab. I wasn't about to bother Lori over the manila envelope. She was too preoccupied. I'd pick it up in the morning when I came over to interview Edith.

Mildred had completed her phone call and headed in my direction. Lori rose from the Devil's Dykes' table and gave her a big hug and kiss. I used the distraction to get out of there before Mildred could change her mind about yours truly, Dickhead. Too many empty beer bottles sat on tables waiting to have their bottoms broken off.

13.

"Last night was awesome," Lori said.

I sat on a stool next to her, at the end of the bar at Big Emma's. I had just returned from a quick trip back to the Oakland PD. Had to give blood and drop off my gun for ballistics testing. The bar was empty, as well it should be at ten-thirty in the morning. Lori had propped open the front door with a mop in an attempt to air it out. I found the odor of stale beer comforting, the smell of my second home.

"Looked like you were having a good time with the bikers."

"Didn't clear them out till 1 A.M. I asked to join the club. But you see there's this sexual orientation problem. I told them I could love a woman. There's so many real bastards out there parading as men, and I keep meeting these women who are just dolls."

"Why don't you?"

"When I see a man that's just my type, I get the hots for him. I start panting."

"Never seen you pant."

"Not literally. Inside I feel like a dog in heat."

"I won't reveal your secret."

"The ladies had some difficulty grasping my feelings on the subject, but they were quite sympathetic. Like I had a disease."

"That was nice of them."

"Oh, they couldn't be sweeter."

"Plan to see them again?"

"You bet. They're going to teach me how to ride a Harley. Then they'll take me out cruising. They said I could be their mascot."

"Well, what will it be next? Now you got the women buzzing around you along with the men."

"You're jealous." She smiled broadly at me. "I can't help it if people like me."

"Help it? You love it."

"Your trouble is you know me too well."

She leaned toward me and gave me a light kiss on the lips. She knew the truth of what I was saying. She needed to be in the center of things, drawing her vitality from those around her. Most people benefited from her attention. Felt warmed, enriched by conversing with a good listener, vicariously revived by a transfusion of Lori's spirit. A win-win situation.

Yet, for me there were times when she could be like a vampire, sucking the life forces out of me so that she could blossom. I felt emptied, invaded. At those times, she was too much for me. I would retreat to my boat and kept out of her way for days at a time. She knew I was hiding out from her. I never expressed my feelings directly to her. Lasting friendship, like love, required placing some limit on confessionals. Too much knowledge of a partner's inner secrets will wreck a relationship every time.

"How are you feeling?" Lori asked me.

"A lot better. Slept well last night. A night out with the ladies can do that for you."

"Would you like to drive with me down to Hegenberger Road this afternoon before the after work crowd shows up?"

"Happy to, but why?"

"Harley's down there."

"Buying a bike this soon? You don't even know how to ride."

"They don't just sell bikes there. Apparel and accessories. I want to get leather pants, a jacket, and a hat like Marlon Brando wore in *The Wild One*."

"You'll look stunning. I wouldn't miss it for the world. But I have an errand to do first. Won't hold us up. I need you to give me that photo you are keeping for me. I want to get it checked out."

"Coming right up."

She retreated to her back office and returned in a minute with a manila envelope in her hand.

"Sandra said I'm not to say a word to you or anybody else about that money business."

Edith Henry sat opposite me in Big Emma's. She wore a man's white shirt, and jeans. We both were sipping coffee. She nibbled on a biscotti. The lunch crowd had begun to gather.

"Like I told Mildred, all I care about is a fellow I call Red. He probably shot Susan but that's none of my business. Now he's out to shoot me. That makes it personal. I'm going to ask you straight out – did you hire a big man who drives a red Saab to watch your stepmother?"

"Mildred said you were on my side."

Edith stared defiantly at me. Dimples on her cheeks softened her intentionally severe image.

"I told her I'd be fair with you. Listen to what you have to say. Help if I could. How'd Sandra work out as a lawyer?"

"She's great. Tough as they come. Had me out of there in minutes. Thanks on that one."

"In return answer my question."

"I don't know anyone like that. And I certainly never hired someone to watch, let alone harm, Susan. For one thing, where would I get the money to pay him?"

"From the estate you will collect on her death. He wouldn't come cheap. He's a professional killer."

"Well, I didn't. I wouldn't even know how to find a hit man. You've got to believe me."

"Who do you think did?"

"Honestly, I don't know. I resented Susan moving in on Dad like that. Then inheriting all the money. I don't care much about material things myself, but I have plans for the girls. I think Mildred told you. But...?"

"But what?"

"Susan told me once that the cops thought she had Dad killed. I had found that hard to believe, and I told her so. She seemed so happy when they got married. Dad, too. His death devastated her. She never drank before."

"Sounds as if you liked her."

"She pissed me off. Yet I felt sorry for her. You know, I think she actually liked me. Never hit on me about the lesbian stuff. Sometimes I felt she was trying to be a real mother to me."

"What did happen to your mother?"

"She died when I was very young. I don't even remember her."

I looked up at her. Her short natural blond hair, razor cut stylishly made her head look too small for her large round gold hoop earrings. She didn't look tough. Quite the opposite – needy. I hadn't suspected Edith felt any affection for Susan. She could be laying it all on for me. Yet somehow it did fit. Brought up without a mother, she had an unfulfilled need that Susan could have connected with. The motorcycle gang was now her family. Mildred was one lucky lady.

"Let me show you something," I said.

I withdrew the gold frame photo from the envelope and handed it to her.

"Do you remember this photo on her desk the night of her death?" I asked.

"No."

"No? Are you sure? It was in her hand when we arrived."

"Wasn't on her desk when I tried to talk with her."

Funny. No reason for Edith to lie. After being shot, she must have used her last moments of life to find the photo. It was as if she was handing me the picture from the grave.

"I've seen it before, of course."

"What did Susan tell you about it?"

"She got it a few days ago. Her mother had passed away. It was shipped with all her personal stuff. She pointed out the woman and told me she was my step-grandmother. I asked about the man. 'Don't know,' she muttered. She seemed frightened. Kinda strange."

"What were you doing at Susan's house Friday night?"

"I told the cops all about that."

Edith wrinkled her nose and stuck out her chin. Her tough look. Didn't work. Her dimples wouldn't go away.

"Well tell me."

"I was making a final try to get an advance on my inheritance."

"Did you call her at Big Emma's to set up the appointment?"

"No."

"Then why did you show up in the middle of the night?"

"I got a phone call."

"From who?"

"Not telling."

"Sooner or later you are going to have to tell. This is a murder investigation and you are up over your eyeballs in it."

"I told the cops I didn't recognize the voice."

"Stupid. Why do you think you were called? Whoever called you must be the same person who called Susan and set her up to be murdered. You were called to place you at the murder scene."

"Shit, he wouldn't."

"But he did. It was your brother Edward. Am I right?"

It was a guess, but it sure in hell made sense.

"Okay. It was Edward. He called saying he wanted both of us to confront her over the money. I got there early."

"You were supposed to arrive after the killing. And take the blame. Your brother was setting you up."

"I... I just can't believe it of Edward. Not the murder thing. Not that he wouldn't kill, if it advanced his interests. It's just that he's so weak. I can't see him doing anything that decisive."

If I could believe Edith, then the brother was now my prime suspect. Her story did make some sense. I needed to see this Edward character and fast. Take his measure. I decided to move on.

"Was Susan alive when you got there?"

"Of course. But she was out of it. Sound asleep at her desk. Snoring actually. I shook her. I was pissed, Edward getting me over there and not showing up, Susan passed out. Then I saw the purse. That's all I'm saying."

"Just one minute. You say Susan was passed out? She was shot when she was sitting upright."

"So maybe she woke up after I left."

Could be. Red wouldn't have bothered to get her upright before shooting. Probably the noise of that bike when she took off.

I felt someone brush against my shoulder. It was a rather large woman in a muumuu making her way to the ladies room. I looked around me for the first time since Edith had arrived. A group of women, sipping lattés, occupied the next booth. Five men in Pacbell uniforms, drinking beer, dominated the far end of the bar. I smelled garlic cooking.

"Got any suggestions for me to work on? You realize you and your brother are the cops' prime suspects because of the money. Edward have any reasons of his own to kill her? Any reasons separately from your joint interest in the inheritance?"

"Susan told me he was fiddling with the books at the plant. Don't let him know I said that."

I could almost hear the wheels turn in Edith's head. She was thinking about her brother. She damned well believed he set her up and got her in the middle of a murder. She had made her decision not to cover for him any more.

"He could have hired that Red guy," she said.

"Edward?"

"Yes. He's too weak to kill somebody on his own but not too weak to hire a killer."

So much for family values.

"Thanks, Edith. You've been very helpful. As long as you've never had any contact with the man in the red Saab, you'll have nothing to fear. However, you better tell the cops who made that phone call that brought you to the house. The longer you wait the more they will think you were in a conspiracy with your brother to kill Susan."

"What about the money?"

"Cop a plea. Sandra's the best. This murder business is far more important."

The room darkened. I looked up. Mildred's large frame blocked the light as she entered Big Emma's. She ignored me, grabbed Edith's hand and dragged her out of the bar. When Edith reached the door, she turned and smiled back at me.

No Time To Mourn

14.

    A Vivaldi flute concerto filled the cabin of the *Sea Wolf* as I sat down to a bottle of Anchor Steam and a green enchilada. My lunch. I took the photo out of the manila envelope and set the picture in front of me on its little easel. I stared into the eyes of Susan's mother, Sara, as I gnawed away on my soggy enchilada. How many hours had Susan spent looking at that same photo? Must have been linked in some fashion to her murder. I didn't see the connection. However, I couldn't drive out of my mind the thought that Susan's last living act was to grab that photo so tight I had to pry her fingers off the frame. Something must be there that I just had not been able to decipher.

    I looked into Sara's face, partially hidden by a veil that was attached to her pillbox hat. Her delicate features set off surprisingly full lips. There was no smile. A cold seductive beauty. The soldier next to her was large, with a broad chest. His face struck me. Hewn from granite. Powerful, rigid, controlling. Proud to possess her. Like the mother, no smile. Strangely glum couple.

    I studied the picture more closely. The adobe structure in the background was vaguely familiar. I had seen something similar. I didn't think it was a home.

Tim Wohlforth

I turned my attention again to the man in the army uniform standing next to Susan's mother. He had a nametag pinned onto his chest. The letters were so blurry I couldn't make out any of them.

As soon as I had seen the picture I knew it would be right up Blowups, Inc.'s alley. It's a photo-finishing shop on Telegraph Avenue run by an elderly Filipino couple. They survived in the world of one-hour finishing staffed by teeny boppers by specializing in massive blow-ups of photos, as well as restoration work. I had used them before to create poster-sized crash scenes for court exhibits.

I found a card in my file under the nav. Joseph and Teresa Galvis. I headed off for the Oakland stretch of Telegraph Avenue.

No way could I miss the Galvises' store. An enormous photo of Elvis Presley covered the outside wall of the gray stand-alone building. A bell rang as I entered the shop. A dusty counter with a glass front was filled with examples of old photos that had been restored. The fetid air smelled of photo chemicals. Behind the counter was a stool, surrounded by three plain white panels facing an old-fashioned camera on a tripod. The Galvises also took passport photos.

A woman with a round body and a warm smile emerged from behind a curtain that covered a doorway leading to a backroom. I assumed it was filled with a darkroom and additional camera equipment. Not a strand of gray hair on her head, nor a wrinkle on her richly textured bronze face. Her thick lips needed no lipstick. She wore a black dress with white lace trim. Gold-framed reading glasses hung around her neck. A beauty when she was younger. A beauty now.

"How can I help you?" she asked. "Oh, you, the one with the bloody pictures."

No Time To Mourn

"Wolf." I handed her one of my cards. I placed the framed photo on the counter. "Something different this time. A real challenge for you. Teresa, isn't it?"

"That's right." She placed her glasses on her nose and looked down at the photo. "Wedding picture."

"What makes you say that?"

"That's a church behind them. Look at the bells. Also I think that's a cross on top of the tower."

"Are you sure? I didn't see the cross. I can see what might be bells."

This woman, who was almost twice my age, had better eyesight than I did. But Teresa could be mistaken about the marriage thing. I needed more detail from the photo to be sure.

"The cross is a guess. Could be a bird flying overhead. Don't worry. We'll blow it up to be positive. They're not very happy. Let me show you something."

She reached down to a lower shelf below the counter and brought out a photo. A young, thinner, beaming Teresa, in a white wedding dress, stood next to a small, smiling man in a Naval uniform.

"Same time period. Look at our faces. You know," her eyes sparkled, "we still smile."

"I can see that. I'd like to know everything you can tell me about this photo, the paper it's printed on, the frame."

"Joseph," she yelled without turning around.

A skinny man, less than five feet tall, with fine features and sensitive quizzical eyes, came in. He had on a rumpled black three-piece suit and wore silver-rimmed glasses. As he stood next to her, I would have sworn the pair stepped right out of one of the tintypes they repaired.

"Joseph's the real expert," Teresa continued. "He knows paper, frames, everything about photography. He's been working at it for more than forty years now."

Joseph picked up the photo in his small wrinkled hands, discolored by years of working with chemicals. He turned the frame over, grabbed a pair of thin-nose pliers from behind the counter, and pried out the small nails holding the backboard. He removed the print paper and felt the edges. A finger traced the faint outline of the word "Kodak" on the back. He turned the photo over, held it at arms' length and moved into a beam of light flooding in from a window.

"Just a guess, mind you. I'd say it was taken in 1946, latest 1947."

"How do you know?"

"The print paper. It's the type not available to us until 1946. Better quality than what we had when I got out of the service in '45. The best went to the armed forces during the war. Also the sepia effect. Very popular then. Now everybody wants pure white. But the giveaway's the edging. See the serration. Kodak used to provide print paper in stock sizes edged that way. By 1948 they dropped that line. We had to trim our own."

"Anything about the frame?"

"Cheap. See?" He held the backboard up and pointed to a little sticker. "Woolworth's. I'd say these people hired a good photographer to take a wedding picture and then went out and got their own frame to save money. People didn't have much in those days, not right after the war. Remember, Teresa?"

"Don't remind me. We lived off greasy garlic noodles." She patted her belly.

"What I need you to do is blow up certain sections of the photo. Play with the contrast. I need as much detail as possible."

"Sounds like fun." Joseph had a wide grin on his little face.

"Joseph worked in a Naval lab during the war," Teresa explained. "Aerial photography."

As Joseph and Teresa bent over the photo, I pointed out the areas I wanted them to concentrate on. I stressed the nametag. Any letters would help. I also asked for blow-ups of the faces of the man and woman.

"The adobe building as well. Teresa says it's a church."

"She knows churches," Joseph said proudly. "Her hobby is taking pictures of old missions, monasteries, religious statues, and the like. That will be her project."

"I'll pay whatever it costs. How long?"

"We're not some one-hour place," Teresa said. "Joseph's a craftsman. Give us a week."

"That long?"

"Check in a few of days."

I knew I couldn't have entrusted this work to better people.

15.

I've been on shopping trips with Lori before. She likes to take me along, not that she pays the slightest attention to my opinions. It is not even so she can have an audience. She gathers one wherever she goes. It's that, at times, Lori likes the feeling of doing the couple thing. So I become the spouse for the day, though not for the night. I must admit I enjoy the bit of play-acting.

I settled into a chair by a full-length mirror at the Harley store, developing a proper husband-type frown. Lori had recruited a salesman and was walking around the store, tossing garments into his overloaded arms. The fellow was thin, head shaved, with silver rings in his two ears and nose. The only other customers were a stocky Hispanic biker, dressed entirely in leather, and his similarly attired, even heavier, dyed-blond wife. We had noticed their matching touring Harleys parked out front, with "Papa" and "Mama" painted in script on their sides.

Lori ducked into a changing booth and reemerged, about ten minutes later, transformed. She wore skintight leather pants, cowboy boots with the Harley logo on them and a man's chambray shirt one size too small for her. Her hat, placed jauntily on the side of her head, was exactly like the one Marlon Brando once wore. I saw she had to remove the ribbon that created her ponytail, allowing her long platinum blond hair to fall straight down her back. The salesman's eyes were about to fall out of their sockets.

"Don't sell many of those hats anymore," the salesman commented, "not since they passed the helmet law."

"Which should I get, a vest like the girls, or maybe the full jacket?"

"The girls?" the salesman asked.

"The Devil's Dykes. Good friends of mine. They recommended your place to me, Teddy." She was already on a first name basis with the fellow.

"Of course," Teddy gulped. "My best customers."

"Let me try the vest. Without a shirt."

The Hispanic biker abandoned the accessory area to watch the show. He ignored his wife's nudges. Lori ducked into the changing booth and bobbed back out in a minute, vest only covering the one section of her body that was not thin.

"Wonderful," I said. The biker couple and Teddy clapped.

"Thanks. That settles it. Vest it is. I may return for a jacket."

Lori changed back into her not particularly shabby street clothes – light blue flared miniskirt, matching blue ribbon holding up her ponytail, white Big Emma's tee shirt, and high heels. She handed Teddy her plastic. He processed her order and placed the new outfit into a shopping bag with "Harley-Davidson" written on the side. We headed for the door and Lori's white Trans-Am. It was her trip and her wheels.

"Let's not go back right away," Lori said. "Look, the fog has cleared. It's such a nice day. How about a walk on the beach at Alameda?"

"Sounds marvelous."

As we climbed into Lori's car, six monster bikes, driven by shaggy hulks, pulled up in front of the store. Hell's Angels. Lori started up the engine and spun her wheels, spewing gravel on the brutes, as she sped out of the Harley-Davidson parking lot. The biker image was affecting her driving. I figured the Angels would roar right after us and run us off the road. But she waved at them and smiled. They laughed and waved back. The Angels were getting soft.

Lori turned left, heading toward the Oakland Airport. She flipped on her radio. The twang of Willie Nelson's singing filled the interior of the Trans-Am.

"Tell me the honest truth. Do you really like my new image?"

"Love it. I love all your images."

She frowned. Had I insulted her? She slowed down the Trans-Am.

"Shall I take the leather back?"

"No. What I mean is you're always playing a role, projecting an image to others. Most people, that's all they see. The beautiful woman with dazzling blue eyes."

"Are you trying to say that I'm just glitz?"

Now I had really put my foot into it. But I stumbled on.

"That's all that most people see. Not me. My friend is that loving creature that lives deep beneath the glitz. Take the way you connect with people, like the women bikers. I can't do that. Can you imagine me going up to those Hell's Angels, slapping backs and passing pills? You extend yourself emotionally to others. Especially to me."

She smiled at me.

"Thanks. I know you mean it. It's just that sometimes I doubt myself. Never was good at school. Attention deficit, it was called. And I somehow never got around to doing the homework. I know I'm attractive. So I have always used my looks to get what I want. I'm not sure that's right."

"You could be some rich dude's trophy wife, but instead you work hard at Big Emma's. You deserve whatever success you have achieved in life."

We had been caught by a red light in airport traffic. The light turned green, and Lori turned her attention to driving. We had said it all anyway. I would have thought Lori was the last person to doubt herself. Live and learn. We started to pass through the intersection.

"Where do we turn?" she asked.

"Here," I said.

Lori swung a right at the last minute. The Trans-Am barreled down a long straight road beside a little used section of the airport. An old skeleton of a World War II bomber lay deserted on the field. Behind it was an abandoned, rusting hangar.

"Isn't that a red car way in the distance behind us?" Lori asked as she glanced into her rearview mirror.

I turned around in my seat and looked out the back window.

"I see nothing."

"Maybe it turned off."

"We're letting Red get to us. About one quarter of the cars on the road are red and they get most of the tickets."

Lori found a parking space along a stretch of the beachfront in Alameda. The section of beach we had chosen to walk on was deserted. It was bordered by private homes. The warm sun caressed us, the air made crisp by the recently retreated fog. How pleasant the Bay Area can be in the Fall.

"You're not going to get very far with those high heels."

"I'll take them off."

"And your stockings?"

"What stockings? I don't go to the tanning salon for nothing."

Lori stooped, took off her high heels, laced them together, and walked toward the water, swinging the shoes in her left hand. I caught up to her and grabbed her right hand. We had the place to ourselves. Way in the distance some dogs ran around a dot of a figure on the public beach. Seagulls swept overhead, while a lively breeze blew a light salty mist into our faces. A group of small racing sailboats tacked in the wind, heading for a red buoy that marked the entrance to the estuary. I could see the tops of the Transamerica Pyramid and the Embarcadero Towers poking out of the fogbank that covered San Francisco.

"You'll get your feet wet," Lori said. "Maybe you should take your shoes off, too."

Lori was already walking in the wet sand. I let go of her hand and took off my shoes and socks. Then I rolled up the cuffs of my pants.

"That's better," Lori said as she danced in front of me. "See the sandpipers? How they follow the receding waves and then run back up the shore to keep out of the deep water. We can do that, too."

The surf on the bay was gentle, not like the ocean. More than a dozen sandpipers scampered methodically in rhythm with the movement of the frothy water, picking at the exposed wet sand with their little beaks. It was as if they had been choreographed. Lori dashed ahead into the bay, like a little girl playing. She stopped when the water reached her knees and called to me.

"Come on. Catch me."

She laughed and ran, splashing in the direction of the public beach. I plunged in after her, getting my jeans wet. She ran faster and faster. I was having trouble catching up. Then she stumbled and fell headlong into the water, coming up in a couple of seconds, soaked. Her wet tee shirt, now transparent, clung to her breasts, accentuating her erect nipples.

Lori stood there laughing so hard I thought she would cry. Then she wrapped her hands around her waist and shivered. She was still holding her shoes. The water was damned cold. I quickened my pace and caught up to her, my pants now thoroughly soaked.

"You're a crazy lady. You know you're no longer some little kid."

"I beat you."

No Time To Mourn

I took her into my arms and massaged her back.

"Let's get back to dry land," I said.

Grabbing her free hand, I tugged her toward the shore. We staggered onto the beach, shaking the water off like dogs, smiling at each other.

The sky darkened, as a dense fog rolled back in, bringing with it frigid air. The fog completely covered the beach. The two of us hugged each other for warmth. Crazy night with the motorcycle gang. Crazy day with Lori. I felt so alive, happy. I wasn't going to allow some cold fog to dampen my good spirits.

I heard the crunch of footsteps on the sand. Someone was coming from the direction of the public beach. I turned from Lori and searched the fog for the trespasser. This beach had become ours.

A phantasm emerged from out of the fogbank, looking more like an animal than a man. It was Red. His must have been that red car back by the airport. He was the lone figure stirring up the dogs when we first arrived on the beach. We had been so preoccupied with the water and each other that we hadn't noticed his progress toward us. Then the fog had covered his final approach.

I glanced around. No one else on the beach. He was no more than ten feet away. We were well within the range of his infernal peashooter. He had found his moment.

The wind blew away the fog cloud that lay between us. I saw him clearly for the first time, as it was still fairly light out. I couldn't keep my eyes off him. His round bald head sank into his barrel frame, revealing no neck at all. Beady eyes pierced through slits of flesh, holding me in their magnetic grip. Water from the mist dripped down his reddened face. I absorbed each detail of his visage like a scientist with a microscope checking out the DNA of a unique strand of the AIDS virus.

He wore a white, wrinkled dress shirt with a stained open collar. Black suspenders held up black pants that had lost their crease long ago and were shiny at the knees. A matching black jacket was slung carelessly over his right arm, barely hiding his automatic. He reminded me of a venomous great-horned toad. I had lifted the wrong rock.

Red said nothing, his eyes absorbing me, watching for my slightest move. He let his coat drop, raised his arm slightly, and took careful aim directly at my heart. A grin formed on his moist lips.

No Time To Mourn

16.
When faced with death, your whole life is supposed to flash through your mind. Not so with me. My mind was blank. I neither thought nor felt anything, not even fear. I couldn't move, held in place by the bastard's stare. In less than a second concern for Lori replaced emptiness. I knew I couldn't save myself, but it was possible I could divert Red's attention and let Lori escape.

I rolled to the right.

"Go," I shouted, hoping she'd dash to the left. She didn't move. She had a better idea.

Lori's shoes smashed into Red's face. He pulled the trigger. He was so close I heard a slap as he fired the shot. The bullet went astray. Lori fell to her knees and started scooping. She blasted him with a hail of sand. He threw up both hands to ward off Lori's blows. Disoriented, he wiped the sand from his eyes.

Lori continued to scoop and fling. I joined in. Red fought with one hand to keep his face clear, while with his other hand he lowered his gun and prepared to shoot again.

"Now!" I shouted.

I rushed directly at Red and hit him with my good shoulder with all my might. It was like colliding with the side of a freight train. I bounced right off him. Lori kicked him in the balls. With bare feet, for Christ's sake.

"Fuck," he shouted.

He wobbled, temporarily losing his balance. He didn't fall down. Guy was built like a brick shit house. He got off a wild shot.

"Run! Run!" I screamed.

We both plowed right past him driving ourselves through the soft sand toward the road. Two more pings. Sand spattered directly in front of me. I couldn't see the bastard in the fog, but he shot like he could see us. I heard him smashing his way through the sand. Then three shots in a row spattered sand around us. He was gaining on us.

We were getting close to the macadam. Four more pings. The bullets whizzed by my ears. He was aiming higher. The sound of glass breaking. A shot must have hit a window in one of the houses on the other side of the road.

That made ten. His little gun couldn't have more bullets than that in its magazine. At least I hoped not. That is, until he had time to stop and put in another clip. As I ran, the bandages that covered my bruised ribs tore against my flesh. I gasped for air but kept running. Pain mingled with pain. Lori was doing more than keeping up with me. She was sprinting ahead.

We hit the macadam, and I looked back. I couldn't see anything. Didn't hear him running either. He must have stopped for a moment to load a new clip into his gun.

"Come on," I yelled to Lori. "We're almost to the car."

That's when we heard the sirens. We both stopped and turned. I heard Red charging in the sand. The sound of his footsteps began to fade. He was running away. We collapsed right there on the pavement. I coughed and wheezed, trying to get my wind back. My ribs and shoulder felt like I was the guy trying to stop the tank in Tiananmen Square and failed. I crawled up to Lori and took her in my arms.

"You saved my life."

No Time To Mourn

"You see," she said gently, "I was right to wear high heels to the beach."

Two Alameda police cars pulled up next to us. A woman patrol officer hopped out of one, her gun drawn. A cop in the other car rolled down a window and held a shotgun aimed at us.

"Now which one of you two shot a bullet into the window of that house over there?" she asked.

"Red did," I said. "He was trying to kill us. Just murdered someone in Oakland. Ran toward the public beach."

She walked over to the edge of the sand and stared out at the fog. Then she returned, shaking her head. "There's no one out there."

How could she be so sure? Even if Red was there, she wouldn't see him.

Lori started to get up.

"Gotta get my shoes," She muttered. "Nordstrom. Cost a fortune."

Then she fell back to the ground. Exhaustion must have finally hit her.

"Me, too." I added. "L.L. Bean's best moccasins."

"You two are going no place," the cop in the car with the shotgun yelled.

The lady cop roughly yanked me to my feet, pulled my arms behind my back and handcuffed me.

"Take those cuffs off him," Lori screamed at the cop. "We're the victims, damn it. We go for a stroll on the beach and get shot at. Then you treat us like criminals."

"Get up, Miss," the cop said.

Lori just glared at her. The cop in the car opened the door and approached us, shotgun leveled at Lori's head. She reluctantly rose to her feet. The lady cop cuffed her.

We were definitely not getting through to this pair. We had some explaining to do.

Tim Wohlforth

It was 9 P.M. when Nina and Ollie walked into Big Emma's. The Alameda police had grilled us for two hours, finally letting us go. The clincher was the bullet. After digging it out of the wall, they identified it as .22 caliber. I had 'em as far as my gun was concerned. Not only was it a .38, but the Oakland PD still had it. They checked with Oakland and Nina helped. Finally, we were allowed to go home and change clothes. No shoes, however. They were being held as evidence.

"Shoes as evidence?" Lori had asked.

"You said your shoes hit this Red fellow in the head," the lady cop responded. "Maybe there's some trace blood or skin from the shooter on your shoes."

She had a point.

Nina and Ollie slid into the booth under Big Emma. Lori and I joined them. My shoulder still ached, as did my ribs. I was not in a great mood to submit to more questioning. Still, I figured it was better to be alive in pain than dead in the sand.

"You two had a close call," Nina started in. "Lori, I hear you were the hero. That sand throwing was smart."

Ollie just sat there glumly. He was not one for compliments.

"Came to me all at once," Lori said. "When we were kids Joe and I would get into sand fighting contests. I've had enough sand thrown in my face to know it really blinds you."

"Does the bullet match?" I asked.

"Too soon to tell," Nina answered. "We suspect it will. Same caliber. Same shooter. But the shooting happened in Alameda and they send their bullets to the Sheriff's Crime Lab. We're coordinating things with them. You got a good look at him?"

"Too good."

His ugly features were etched in my memory. I described Red for them.

"Not a very attractive dude," Nina noted. "Found his jacket."

"Fantastic. That's got to be a lead."

"Label torn out. Nothing in the pockets. Guy doesn't take chances."

"His luck has got to end soon."

Nina just nodded and turned toward her partner.

"Ollie, I believe you have something to say."

She nudged him with her elbow. The place was mobbed. Most of the patrons had already downed a couple. Good spirits were leading to laughter, shouts, slaps on backs, ribbing, the clink of glasses, and the banging of dice cups. I leaned closer to hear him.

"Well, it does appear that the two of you are in grave danger. Miss Mazzetti as well as Wolf. This will require a change of strategy on our part. We plan to place both of you under twenty-four hour surveillance. It will be an undercover operation because we want to catch Red, not just scare him away."

"Kind of late," Lori said. "He almost killed us."

Ollie shrugged his shoulders. The man was all heart.

He continued. "Wolf, remember what I said at our last meeting. Keep away from the Susan Henry murder investigation. Or else."

"Come on. I wasn't investigating Susan. We go for a walk on the beach and the bastard shoots at us."

"And why did he shoot at you?" Ollie continued.

"Why don't you find him and ask him?"

I was getting no place with this lame brain.

"That's precisely what we intend to do," Nina intervened. "You two stay put. He goes after you, we catch him. If either of you go any place, like even to Safeway, you call. Got it?"

"We promise," Lori said.

"The lady speaks for you, Jim?" Nina asked.

"Absolutely," I said. "So we're the bait now. We're supposed to sit around and hope you guys spot Red before he shoots us."

"You got it," Ollie said.

He got up from the table and stomped out of the place. Nina shrugged her shoulders, smiled, and followed him into the night. Lori and I sat there for a few minutes, saying nothing. The noise from the bar surrounded me like the sound system in an IMAX theater. I felt as if I were a live rabbit tethered to a tree as bait for a jaguar. Lori pressed her thin frame against me. I knew she was thinking the same thought.

"The cops are useless," I said to her. "But don't worry. You can count on me."

"And who saved us out at the beach?"

She had a point.

"Do me a favor," she continued.

"Anything."

"Buy me a new pair of shoes and then place razor blades in the high heels."

Tough chick.

17.

I didn't sleep well that night. I ached all over. Motrins weren't doing anything for me. However, I spent the time usefully. I mulled the case over and over in my mind, the danger I had placed Lori in, my options. The attack on the beach had been spontaneous. He followed us, looking for his opening. We stupidly supplied him with one. He made his move and failed.

He would scurry back under his rock. He'd get another jacket, reload his gun, and plan his next move. He knew we would take precautionary measures. His next effort would be meticulously planned and executed. He was a pro.

I was shitty at the waiting game. I was sure Oakland PD would do its best to protect us. Red, however, could bide his time and wait for the cops to get sloppy. Or he could wait even longer until the cops got tired of watching us. Then move in for the kill. He was in charge. He called the shots. When. Where. How. I couldn't accept that.

I was a proactive kind of guy. I had to return to the hunt, find that damned rock, turn it over, expose the bastard to daylight, and grind him into the ground with my foot. There was only one way to do this – find the person or persons who hired Red. Then follow him/her/them to Red. That wouldn't be easy but it was doable. I had already gotten some information from Swineheart and from Edith. But I needed more. So much more.

I spent the next morning and early afternoon working on my computer. Not my cup of tea. I preferred action. Somehow sitting in front of a computer seemed just like the desk job I thought I could avoid by being a private eye. Yet, I found I was spending more time these days in front of a computer screen than wearing down the gum on my shoes. Luckily, I was damned good at it.

I had on CD-ROM a complete national phone list as well as street maps of every town in the United States. I found the Social Security Master Death Index, another CD-ROM, quite useful. The government created an SS number for each person when they go to work. When they die, this number was added to the Death Index. It was never recycled. That was the quickest way to find out if a search subject was still alive.

I belonged to a private Internet data base service available only to licensed PIs and lawyers. It could produce detailed information, gathered from thousands of data bases, on ninety million Americans. Then there was *LexisNexis*. It's quite expensive but well worth it. The service was a massive database of court records, newspapers and other printed media. If the target ever appeared before a judge or had made it into print, I'd find the information. Saved digging into courthouse records directly or newspaper morgues.

I also subscribed, indirectly, to several credit raters. Setting this up took a bit of doing because we shamuses were not allowed access to their services. Ever hear of Jack London Yacht Brokers? I must admit I haven't been doing much business since I filled out a Fictitious Business Name form at the County Clerk's Office, but I've been making a number of credit checks.

No Time To Mourn

I deeply believed in the right to privacy. I didn't think the IRS, the FBI, and ATF, or the cops had a right to snoop on anyone. Keep big Government out of our living rooms, bedrooms, trash and business files. So why did I earn my living digging out other people's secrets? I was a hypocrite.

I ran the name Edward Henry, both with and without the Junior, through my data bases and began collecting information. At first, I didn't get back much that was useful. Henry was a common name, and a good search required some additional information. I had his place of residence but I really needed an SS number or date of birth.

LexisNexis came to the rescue. It produced the original stories on the Henry murder as well as an obit. The latter furnished date and place of birth, as well as some good bio material. Soon my system was spewing out mounds of information.

I printed it all out and placed the results on my table. I stuck a CD by the Tallis Scholars — now that's obscure — in the player, made myself a cup of French roast, and settled down to work. There was a slight breeze on the estuary and *Sea Wolf* rocked gently in its slip. Occasionally I could hear a cabin cruiser passing in the distance. Monty had buried herself in her rocks and was asleep. Luckily, pythons didn't snore. One advantage over a human mate.

Taking out a lined yellow pad, I started making notes. Before long I had a pretty complete dossier on Senior. He had been born in Boston, Massachusetts. His father was a history professor at Harvard and his mother a practicing psychiatrist. He had graduated from MIT in 1958 with an MBA. Got married the same year. Worked in printing management in the Boston area until 1968. He moved out here and bought his present house in Crocker-Highlands. Even then it must have cost mega-bucks. The guy must have done well in printing in Boston or maybe his parents died and he inherited a pile. I could find that out, but who cared.

Tim Wohlforth

When he arrived in Oakland, he founded Color Graphics in partnership with somebody named Jonathan Stanwell. The two ended up in court in 1985, suing each other. It went to arbitration and Edward bought out Stanwell's interest for one million dollars, most of it borrowed. He must have prospered since then because, by the time of his death, he had a top credit rating. The house was paid off as well.

Edward, Jr. was born in 1970 and Edith in 1975. The mother passed away in 1980. Breast cancer. Junior was the guy that interested me. I would bet the little that was left from the grand Susan gave me he was the key to the whole case. He got the computer's royal treatment.

A credit check on Edward, Jr. was more than suspicious. He was in arrears on his credit cards. There was a recently issued credit alert on Color Graphics. Edith had suspected as much. She was right. Where had all the money gone so quickly after papa's death? I was going to have to ask Junior some tough questions.

It was very important to carry out any investigation systematically. I knew I had been stumbling along on this one. I had allowed Red to get under my skin and this had affected my normally methodical approach. I created three files out of the mess on my table. The first included all the historical material on the senior Henry as well as my handwritten summary. The information of Junior went into a second file. I saved the reports from *Nexis* on old man Henry's murder for a third file.

It was time to digest what I had learned so far. I now knew that the murders of Edward and Susan were linked and that Red pulled the trigger. Who hired Red? I had three scenarios and four suspects. I wrote them down on my yellow pad:

<u>Scenario one:</u> If Red's target was Edward alone, then the only possible candidate for his boss would be Susan. Edward's death benefited only her. She became a wealthy woman and freed of an older husband. This scenario required me to believe either she hired Red because she wanted to commit suicide, but

couldn't pull the trigger herself. Or she hired him to kill her husband, but failed to pay him off. Then he returned to take her out. Crazy. Not the Susan I knew.

Scenario two: If the elder Edward and Susan were the targets, the children are great candidates. This certainly made a lot of sense. According to this scenario, Red tried to bump them both off and succeeded at first only with Edward. Then he returned to take out Susan. Junior and Edith could have conspired together to hire Red to carry out the crime, planning to split the inheritance. This was consistent with the phone call made to Susan. Edith's turning up at the scene of the murder suggested a variant. Edward acted alone. I tended to believe Edith. Junior, therefore, seemed the more likely of the two. He had the additional motive of covering up hanky panky at Color Graphics.

Scenario three: If Susan alone was Red's original intended victim, it was hard to see how Junior or Edith would benefit from her death. She had no money of her own. It was possible that a fourth, as yet unknown, person, linked in some fashion to Susan's past, was Red's boss. Susan deeply believed in this scenario. This was why she insisted on telling me about the photo and reached for it in her last moments of life. I was convinced she had additional reasons to come to that conclusion. Reasons she held back from me. Something she knew gave that photo special potency.

Suspect one: Susan. See scenario one.
Suspect two: Edith. See scenario two.
Suspect three: Junior. See scenario two.
Suspect four: Unknown. See scenario three.

I filed away my list, knowing full well I might never look at it again. Its purpose was to organize my own thinking. Hopefully this would lead me to organize my actions. There was no way to pursue scenario one and suspect one. Susan was not available for an interview. I had already interviewed suspect two, Edith.

Tim Wohlforth

Next on my very short list of suspects to interview was Junior. Five million dollars was a lot of temptation. I wanted some answers about the phone call business. And about his finances. I didn't want to tackle him without some ammunition, something more than his weak credit rating.

That's when I thought of Howie Steiner. He was a recently divorced middle-aged man who viewed himself as some kind of stud. He wore a heavy gold chain around his neck, had a fat diamond-studded gold ring on his left pinky, dyed his hair a little too red, and leered at all the twenty-something ladies at Big Emma's. Sold paper and hit the place most every day around five o'clock, after he had completed his rounds of print shops. Not my favorite kind of guy.

One evening he bent my ear for over an hour about the printing industry in the Bay Area. The place happened to be bereft of single women. I was all he had to talk to. Bankruptcy was widespread in the industry, he explained. Credit was easily available and companies over expanded in good times only to go belly up when the market tightened. The paper vendors, who sold on credit, watched the owners like hawks. They shared info among themselves. Howie would know what's going on with Color Graphics.

My next step was to buy a drink for a man with a gold chain around his neck and a fat gold ring on his baby finger.

18.

I found Howie Steiner at the far end of the bar, away from the entrance. The only single woman customer left in the place had just patted him on the shoulder, in a kind of motherly fashion, and headed out the door. It was a good time to strike.

"How about a drink? I've run into something right up your alley."

He wore a sport shirt, covered with fishing boats alternating with "Cabo San Lucas" in script. It was open half way down, exposing his hairy chest and a gold chain.

"Young, pretty, big tits?"

"Business, Howie, business."

His face dropped. A brown engraved Mexican belt with a silver buckle, pulled tight below his belly, held up tan gabardine cuff-less slacks. Dark brown embroidery covered the seam on both sides of the trousers. I steered him to my booth beneath Big Emma and ordered our drinks, Oban for me and a martini for Howie. Alice waited on us. She worked part-time at Big Emma's. A middle-aged, single mother with two daughters in parochial school, she was a hard worker with a sunny disposition. Lori sat at the bar watching women's basketball on ESPN.

"Ever hear of Color Graphics?"

"Of course, used to be one of my best customers. Old Ed Henry and I were like brothers."

"You said 'used to.' What happened?"

"I've heard about the wife's death. You involved somehow?"

"Yeah."

I gave Howie a short version of the events of the past few days. He looked impressed.

"Exciting job you got there. Mine's dullsville. The girls must be all over you, like James Bond. Beginning with *Numero Uno* over there." He waved a heavy gold ringed finger in Lori's direction and winked. I gave him my man-about-town smile and returned the discussion to business.

"You were telling me about Color Graphics?"

"This is all in confidence. *Mano a mano*, buddy."

I believed Howie was trying to say "man to man" rather than "hand to hand." His phony Spanish was wearing me down, but I had to play him.

"*Tenga la seguridad,*" I replied. That means "rest assured." Howie gave me a quizzical look, but he was not about to admit he didn't understand what I said.

"Color Graphics had a fine reputation under the old man. Top credit rating. The guy's word was as good as a signed contract. He'd just pick up the phone and call me. I'd ship him a carload of paper without so much as consulting our accounting department. We're talkin' tens of thousands of dollars. I was doing almost a million dollars a year with him in paper and supplies. The commission covered a lot of martinis. But Junior's a different kind of animal."

"What do you mean?"

"The old man turned purchasing over to the kid the last year before he got killed. Trying to break him in to take over the plant. Once Edward married Susan his mind was no longer into business. He was crazy about that broad. I met her when she was down at the plant. Charming. Nice figure for a middle-aged woman."

No Time To Mourn

"You liked her?"

"Well, yes, of course. She's not my type. Sort of artsy-fartsy, if you know what I mean." Howie gave me a broad wink and then scanned the bar, checking if a female of the species might have snuck in. "That was part of her charm for Edward."

"So you don't think it was likely she had him killed?"

"You think that?"

"No, but the cops do."

"I'm in the people business, *hombre*. Learned over the years how to judge 'em. I'm seldom wrong. That lady was no killer."

"Tell me more about the elder Edward and Junior."

"I took the old man out to lunch after the two got back from their honeymoon. Changed person, relaxed, all smiles. He told me all he wanted to do with the rest of his life was spend time with her, traveling. He wanted me to steer young Eddie in the right direction so he could take the business over. I know the trade. Been my life for thirty years, *compañero*. He chose the right man."

"Speaking of traveling, been to Mexico recently?"

"Just got back. How'd you guess."

"I'm a detective."

"Impressive."

I caught Alice's eye and held up two fingers. I needed to keep Howie lubricated. Lori was still glued to the tube. No new customers had entered the bar.

"You were telling me about the son," I continued.

"Eddie's bent."

"In what way?"

"He approached me on a kickback scheme. Told me to add a dollar a hundred weight to all my prices, and return fifty cents to him in cash. He said papa would never catch on. When you're buying paper by the ton, the *pesos* add up."

"Do you know what he wanted the money for?"

"Gambling. The guy's into horses. Got a bookie in Reno. He's lousy at it."

"Did you do it?" I asked.

Alice showed up, took our empty glasses and placed fresh drinks in front of us. With short curly brown hair, and a touch of freckles on her face, I pictured her on an Iowa farm baking a pie with a wood stove. She gave Howie's shoulder a matronly squeeze. About all the action the chap was getting that evening.

"Are you kidding?" Howie was genuinely taken aback by my question. He had his code of honor. "My company would never go for it. Anybody can take an order, so I live on my reputation. I don't do under the table deals."

"Did you tell the father?"

"Not directly. I hadn't the heart. I did suggest Junior needed direct supervision for awhile."

"What's going on now?"

"You won't tell anybody where you got this information, *compañero*? Even if they put your head in a vise?"

"Got my word. *La Verdad.*"

Howie leaned forward and almost knocked me over with his 100 proof breath. Though there was no one within ten feet of our booth, he spoke in a whisper and out of the side of his mouth.

"No sooner was the old man under the ground and Eddie started placing carload orders for web stock. That's the paper that comes in rolls and runs on the really big presses. Color Graphics doesn't own web presses. Then he told me to ship the stuff to Sparks, Nevada. A lot of printers and warehouses are out there."

"Why would he do that?"

"Precisely what I asked him. Said he was speculating on the paper price. Holding the paper in Nevada where there's no inventory tax, then he planned to resell it in California and make a bundle."

"Makes some sense."

"Not when the price of paper is falling. The guy's not dumb. There was something more involved. So I made some inquiries through our Reno office. Quiet like. *Silencio.*"

"What did you find out?"

"He was shipping the paper to a printing plant, Enterprise Web, not a warehouse. He's a part owner of the plant. Get it?"

"Not entirely."

"Took me a little while, too. Guy's a real *bandito*."

Junior was just the executor of the old man's estate, Howie explained. It belongs, or belonged, to Susan. Upon her death, Junior would have to split it with the sister. So Junior bought paper, charged Color Graphics, and shipped the paper to Enterprise Web. Color Graphics started losing money while Enterprise made whopping profits printing jobs with free paper.

"Paper can account for more than fifty percent of the cost of a job, especially long run web work," he explained.

While the property Junior had to share with the sister headed into bankruptcy, his new and very private investment prospered.

"Guy's not *loco. Claro?*"

"Who owns the other part of Enterprise?"

"*Bueno.* That's the multi-million dollar question. You're one hell of a detective."

Howie was into his second martini, and the alcohol was going to his head. Fine with me. The more he drank, the more he talked. His way of building up his own self-esteem.

"I asked all my sources in Nevada," he continued. "After thirty years in the trade, I know everybody and everything. But this time I came up empty. Guess what it means in Nevada when you get no answers?"

"What?"

Howie leaned over the table and almost fell upon me. His face contorted into what he must have thought was a wink. I was hit by a blast of breath carrying enough alcohol to break a state trooper's meter. He whispered, "The mob."

"Fits. Thanks. You've been fantastic, *Amigo.*"

"Glad to help." He pressed his finger to his lips and winked again. The winks were beginning to irritate me more than the fractured Spanish. "Remember. *Silencio.*"

"Just one more thing."

"Anything for a *compañero.*"

"Can you fill me in a little about OSHA? The kinds of things they inspect in a plant."

"Why?"

Mimicking Howie, I pressed a finger to my lips. He nodded sagely and gave me a ten-minute lecture on the ins and outs of plant safety inspection. I asked him for Enterprise's address. He dug a little black book out of his pocket, leafed through gold-edged pages, and gave me an address on Pyramid Lake Road. I was surprised the book contained anything outside of women's names.

I got up from the booth, slapped Howie on the back, and sauntered over toward Lori. Howie followed me out of the booth, a little wobbly on his legs, and headed for the front door.

Sad really, when I thought about it. For all his bravado, the guy was needy. The kind that runs with the pack. He spent all day wandering from printing plant to printing plant. At each stop he'd call everybody by their first name, glad-hand them, and slap a few backs. He knew who followed the Raiders, who liked the Niners, which one relished an off-color joke, where it was safer to be politically correct. If his customer liked fishing, he had a favorite lake in the Sierras to recommend. A newborn child? Howie remembered his own kid's first days. There was always a box of See's candies for the secretary on her birthday. Then a long three-martini lunch with a favored customer.

When the business day ended, Howie headed for Big Emma's, hoping to pick up a skirt. What was he really after? Sex? Sure. Stroking his ego through conquest? Definitely. I had a feeling about people like Howie. They needed more. He feared ever being alone, outside the pack, isolated from his community. He might have to get to know himself and not like what he learned. That night he had no choice.

Was my life that much better? I liked to think so. Being an outsider was my thing. I didn't follow sports. I didn't remember jokes. I enjoyed being by myself, tucked into my berth on my cozy boat, listening to Bach, and reading a book. Monty was good enough company for me. She didn't pretend to speak Spanish.

Howie stood for a minute in the doorway. He looked around the bar and smiled weakly. Alice blew him a kiss. Lori was absorbed with her TV. He looked old beyond his years as he staggered unaccompanied out of Big Emma's.

19.

I had one stop to make before I confronted Edward. I went by Oakland PD and picked up my gun. I sensed I would soon need it. The pressure of the pistol in its holster next to my armpit acted like a reality check.

Color Graphics filled half a block in a warehouse district off of Interstate 880 in San Leandro. A dozen cars were parked in the lot beside the plant. Two trucks, with the Color Graphics logo on their sides, and a long semi from a paper mill were pulled up at shipping bays. No two-bit operation.

I walked through the glass doors into the carpeted reception area. Framed awards from printing associations hung on the walls. *Newsweek, Business Week, The Wall Street Journal,* and various printing trade publications covered a low table surrounded by a sofa and two chairs. At first I saw no one behind the high paneled receptionist's cube that dominated the center of the room. Then I spotted a young Asian woman, with perfectly manicured nails and a headset clamped over her neat short black hair. I waited until she had completed her business. She looked up at me.

"How can I help you?"

"I'd like to see Edward Henry."

"Do you have an appointment?"

"No, I don't."

"Your name?" she asked, her voice frosty.

"Wolf."

She pressed some buttons on the phone panel on her desk, repeated the information I had given her to someone at the other end, and then turned to me.

"May I inquire as to the nature of your business with Mr. Henry?"

"Just tell him it concerns Sparks, Nevada."

She repeated my words over the phone, and then smiled coolly at me.

"Mr. Henry will be right out."

In two minutes a worried Edward came through a door next to the receptionist's cube. I could hear the roar of presses from behind him. He wore glasses with thin black rims, a gray suit, a white shirt with blue banker's stripes, and a red and black bow tie. Definitely a resemblance to Sheila's Microsoft friend.

"Would you come this way, Mr. Wolf? My administrative assistant is out sick today."

We walked directly into the plant area. Several large Heidelberg presses stood in a row along the side of the plant facing the shipping bays. Smaller presses lined the other side. Workmen in identical white uniforms swarmed over the gray hulks of metal like maggots on rotted meat. Two forklifts moved blank paper to the machines and printed sheets toward a bindery in the distance. The noise was deafening. I wondered how the pressmen could cope with it until I spotted the earplugs they were wearing.

Edward led me upstairs to an office that had been built out over the plant work area. He opened a door and we entered a small room with a secretary's desk. When he closed the door the noise of the presses disappeared.

"Dad's idea. He liked to view the plant in operation at all times. He didn't need some foreman to tell him when the plant was slow. Just as important, he wanted the employees to see him. I've left everything the way he had it."

He led me into his large, well-appointed office. A Mozart piano concerto floated through the room. Original paintings of California seascapes covered the walls. The elder Edward was a class act.

Junior settled in behind his father's large mahogany desk and fiddled with his pen set. He looked like a little boy playing at being papa. I sat in a chair beside the desk and slid my card over to him.

"You're the guy who found Susan's body. Read about you in the papers."

"That's me."

"So why did you mention Sparks to Esther?"

"Because I know about Enterprise Printing."

A slight tick on the left side of his face revealed fear. Junior was no actor.

"You think you can blackmail me? That would not be very wise. I have friends who don't like blackmailers."

"You're not very discriminating in your choice of friends."

Edward sat rigidly and tapped his pen. Tap, tap, tap. It was getting on my nerves.

"Let's discuss paper," I continued, "paid for by Color Graphics, you've been shipping to Enterprise Printing."

"Who told you that?"

"It's true, isn't it?"

"What's your angle?"

Edward made an effort at looking tough. The net effect was to make him look like he was going to throw up.

"I'd like to know who murdered Susan."

"I told the cops the answer to that one. It seems obvious to me that Susan hired this guy to kill Dad. Now maybe she didn't pay him or something. So he comes back."

"Do you have any evidence?" I asked.

"Not exactly, but it makes sense, doesn't it?"

"It also makes sense that you had Susan killed to stop her from having the estate audited."

"Make that accusation in public and I'll sue you."

No Time To Mourn

"Did you make a call to Susan at Big Emma's the night she was murdered?"

"Of course not."

The guy was a lousy liar. He visibly shook. His face reddened and he refused to look up at me.

"Did you call your sister, Edith, and ask her to meet you at Susan's house?"

"She say that?"

He looked up angrily at me.

"Yes."

"Then she's a damned liar. Bet she was the one who called Susan. Always trying to get money for her dyke friends."

"I thought Susan was responsible for her own death."

"If it wasn't Susan, it was Edith."

What a family.

"Do you know a large man with a red face who drives a red Saab?"

"You're getting yourself into something way over your head." Edward rose from his seat. "Now get out of here."

"How can you be so sure your partners in Nevada didn't arrange for Susan's murder without telling you?" He squeezed his pencil so hard it broke in two. I had hit pay dirt. "You're the one who may be in over your head."

I walked out of the office and into the organized mayhem of the plant.

My next stop was Fast Press on Lakeshore Avenue. John Grady, who owns the place, prints up whatever I want quickly and without questions. I explained I needed two different business cards by that afternoon.

"Are you crazy?" John said. "The ink won't be dry."

"Slip sheet 'em. Can settle for a couple of each."

I handed him a form letter. "Scan in this logo."

"You're not serious? You could get me in deep shit."
"I take full responsibility. Your name will never come up."
"That logo will be tricky, not to mention illegal."
"Nobody looks closely at logos. I'll pay double."
"Triple."
"You got a deal."

I pulled myself up on the bar stool next to Lori. She was going to be my cover for a trip to Nevada. I knew I would have no trouble signing her on.

"How'd your interview with Edward go?" she asked.

"With the ammunition I got from Howie I had the guy shaking in his boots."

I filled Lori in on both my discussion with Howie and the trip to Edward's printing plant.

"Edward, gambling, Nevada, the mob," she said. "It all fits. Yes, the mob. Red, the professional hit man. Edward's our man."

"What about Edith?"

"Couldn't be. She's just like Ellen. Wouldn't hurt a fly."

"Ellen who?"

"Ellen Degeneres. The TV show. Boy, are you dumb. The whole world knows who Ellen is. I was glued to the tube the night when she came out."

"What has she got to do with Edith?"

"Lesbian, thin, blond, short hair. The same, and Ellen's a sweetheart." She gave me her serious look, eyes wide-open, just a wrinkle on her brow, and then continued, "Edward's different."

"You may be right."

"Tell you something else. Bet Red bought his Saab in Nevada. That's why they can't trace it."

No Time To Mourn

"That's right," I said. "He drives the car into California, replacing the Nevada plates with stolen local ones. No wonder he wasn't worried about anyone identifying his Saab. Clever. Still…"

"You're a hard man to satisfy," Lori said

"Edward has got to be the one who hired Red. It makes such sense. Motive. The mob connection. The phone call. Yet, I can't quite figure out how this photo business fits in. Kind of like a piece of a puzzle that you feel like trimming with scissors to get it in the space where you think it belongs. Trim away as I might, I'm damned if I can fit the photo into the same puzzle that contains Edward."

I turned from Lori to check out Big Emma's. A lone figure had entered, unnoticed, and was now nursing a drink at the end of the bar.

"Isn't that Marcus Welby back there?" I asked.

"Come on."

"The doctor from Highland."

"Oh, Eric."

Her face lit up. She prepared to go down to greet him. Then she noticed my expression. I did my best to hide my disappointment at the fellow's arrival. I didn't succeed. I had no right to be jealous and certainly no claim on her sex life. I wanted her to be happy, to be Lori. But, I'm a human being. I wondered how the Mormon wives handled it in the days before the Second Revelation?

"I'll see if he knows a nurse," she said.

"Don't worry about me. After working all day in the emergency room that fellow needs comforting. And no one comforts better than you."

She gave me a kiss on the cheek and her warmest smile.

"Tomorrow," I said, "I was thinking of taking a little trip to Nevada. The gaming tables."

"Right. As well as a tour of the state's printing facilities. I'm going with you."

"I was counting on that."

"We promised Nina we would let her know if we went any place."

"Of course we'll tell her we're taking a little trip. What happens to us out of state isn't her responsibility."

"Jim?"

"Yes, Lori?"

"And what's going to happen to us?"

20.

It was two o'clock in the afternoon when Lori and I zipped past Reno, took the Sparks off-ramp and left Interstate 80. We went along a road lined with small casinos that paralleled the freeway. I guessed the temperature at 110°. Luckily my Taurus had air conditioning. Lori had kept us entertained during the four-hour drive with a lengthy account of the love life of her cousin Sheri Bendini.

"If having an affair with a married man causes her such anxiety, why doesn't she just break up with him?" I asked. "I've seen her. She'd have no problem finding a single man."

"Exactly my sentiment. I says, 'Hello, anybody home?' But she didn't get it. You know why?"

"Why?"

"Now don't you ever tell her I said this. She enjoys the drama of it all. I don't think she could be happy if she wasn't in some crisis or other."

"Makes you almost feel sorry for the guy."

"Yeah, real sorry. Tears down the cheek sorry. Getting it at home and then over at Sheri's place. Rough life."

"There's Pyramid Lake Road."

I turned left past a small casino with about a dozen cars in front, mostly California plates, and entered a residential area. Air conditioners stuck out of the roofs of the homes.

Occasionally the blue of a swimming pool could be seen in a backyard. We passed a Safeway supermarket, then a large Baptist church. No one was out strolling because of the heat. I had this image of casino towns like Sparks, Reno, and Vegas, as places populated by bettors only, going at it twenty-four hours a day. Yet ordinary people lived along this street in small ranch houses.

I drove six blocks. The homes gave way to a series of trailer parks and an occasional gas station with a mini-mart. We entered an industrial area, passing a large trucking firm and a food wholesaler's warehouse. The desert began, patches of brownish grass, sand, rich green creosote trees, dusty gnarled mesquite, and the occasional ocotillo cactus. The road was perfectly straight and appeared to go on forever, lifting into the sky. In the hazy distance I could make out the outlines of a mountain range.

"You sure we didn't pass the place?" Lori asked. "I mean we're really in the boondocks. It's spooking me."

"Not yet. It is getting kind of desolate. Wait. See way up there on the left?" I spotted a low concrete building set back from the road about half a mile ahead of us. "Must be it."

As we approached I could see that the facility was large, perhaps twice the size of Color Graphics. Surrounded by a chain fence with barbed wire running along the top, the facility looked more like a maximum security prison than a manufacturing plant. We caught up with a huge semi with State of Washington plates. It slowed and prepared to enter the plant gate. As the truck turned, I noticed "Olympia Mills" lettered on the side. I wondered if Howie's firm had set up the shipment.

Two guards swung the huge gates open. One approached the cab of the truck. The driver handed out some papers, the guard nodded his head, gave the papers back, and waved the truck in.

I gunned the engine of my Taurus, hoping to pass right through after the truck. No such luck. The guard who had opened the gate dashed in front of my car, holding up his left hand. His right hand rested on a revolver – looked like a Colt .44 Magnum – that was in a holster on his belt.

He unbuckled the strap holding down the weapon. He pulled the gun from out of its holster and leveled it at me. The other guard gestured for him to lower his weapon. He approached my window.

"May I ask what your business is?"

"This is Enterprise Printing?"

"Yes."

"We're from OSHA." I handed him my card.

"What the hell is OSHA?"

"What you pay your taxes for." The look on the guy's face suggested he was not a happy taxpayer. "Occupation Safety & Health Administration. We're here to inspect the plant."

"Do you have an appointment?"

"Of course not. That's the whole point. If we called ahead of time, you'd have a chance to cover up any possible safety problems. The law requires unannounced inspections. We're going through."

Before he could digest fully what I had said, I gunned the engine and started moving. The guard in front of us jumped out of the way while raising his pistol and aiming directly at us. But the other guard gestured for him to lower the gun again. He called someone on a walkie-talkie.

"So far so good," I said to Lori.

"Great fun, the way you talked down that guy. The gun and all."

"Now we've got to get into that plant and get out fast. I don't like the feel of this place. Got your clipboard?"

"Yes, sir! What are we after when we get inside?"

"I'm not sure. All these armed guards tell us something. Most unusual for an ordinary printing plant. Maybe when we're inside we'll get a better idea of why they're so determined to keep the public at bay. That will help us understand what Edward has gotten himself involved in."

"Got it. Then we'll have motivation for the scumbag bumping off Susan."

As we drove down a long road leading to the plant I noticed on our right a gray helicopter sitting on a tarmac. Two more guards came running out of the main door of the building as we approached. I pulled into a clearly labeled no-parking zone, hopped out of the car holding a briefcase, and grabbed the hand of the first guard to reach me. The heat was staggering. I thought I had walked into a cremation oven.

"I'm Jim Smith, OHSA. That's my assistant Lori Martin in the car. If you've been abiding by the law, there will be no problems at all. Just routine. Won't affect your work schedule."

I brushed past him and pushed the door open leading into the building. Lori rushed after me, her most fetching smile on her face. She wore a tailored tight-fitting conservative blue suit, and was pressing her clipboard against her chest. We walked into a waiting room.

The receptionist rose from behind a counter and tried to head us off. I suspected she was the one at the other end of the walkie-talkie discussion. She had bright red hair piled on top of her head beehive style and wore too much makeup. She looked like she was casting for The Simpsons. She wore a tan-fringed leather vest and mini-skirt, with matching cowboy boots. We were definitely in Nevada.

We brushed past her before she could stop us. Hoping the place was designed like Color Graphics, I plowed through a door next to the receptionist's desk. I guessed right. It led directly into the plant.

The pressroom was enormous. Two huge web presses extended for over fifty feet. In the distance large rolls of paper spun on spindles. The paper passed through a series of stabilizing rollers, ten printing units, a large oven area that dried the ink, finally reaching our end of the plant. In front of us the web of paper, covered with bright glossy printing, was whizzing down a chute toward a complicated folding mechanism. The paper flew by too fast to make out what they were printing. Finished magazine sections shot out of the side of the folder. A conveyor belt fed them into a baler that strapped them. Men picked up the bales and placed them on skids. The noise made Color Graphics by comparison seem like the quiet room in a library. The web presses were on the verge of breaking the sound barrier.

I slipped on some loose wastepaper that was scattered on the floor and fell to the ground. Not a very clean plant. As I picked myself up, I let out a gasp. I had landed in the midst of a pile of pornographic magazine sections. *Dungeon Masters* was the title of one magazine. It pictured a nude man with a very long dong, pierced by a rusty nail. Three naked men, holding whips, hovered over him. His back was covered with blood. I reached down, grabbed a signature and stuffed it into my briefcase. Underneath it was a pedophile magazine. A middle-aged man was screwing a prepubescent girl. Another magazine featured a naked boy, around eight years old, giving a blow job to a balding man. I shoved those pages also into my satchel. Two burly men in brown suits walked toward me. Had they seen me take the sheets?

"What's this all about?" one of them snarled at me.

"OSHA. Show me your MSDSes."

I had to shout to be heard over the roar of the presses. The pressmen were ignoring us, running up and down besides the great whale-like structures, as signatures flew out the end. My eyes stung from chemical fumes. Despite air conditioning, heat radiated from the drying ovens.

"What are you talking about?"

"You need a sheet on every chemical you use, like blanket wash, even the inks. It's got to be available to all employees."

"Of course, of course."

"And the minutes of your Safety Committee?"

"Safety Committee?"

"You have one, I assume? It's required by law."

"How are we supposed to know?" the gruff brown-suited man asked. The other one hadn't said a word so far.

"That's your responsibility. Congress passes the law. We enforce it. Your job is to familiarize yourself with its requirements."

My voice was getting hoarse competing with the presses.

"Why don't we all retire to my office and talk over this matter?" The other brown suit finally spoke in a carefully intoned cultured voice. So he was the boss. "I'm sure we could come to some accommodation."

"Fine. But first Miss Martin and I need to look over the plant for safety hazards. You should sweep up the place. I slipped myself. Miss Martin has noted that."

"Ernie," Smoothy spoke to the gruff one, "please assist these people in their inspections. This is a working plant and we would not wish them to inadvertently get injured. Then bring them to my office." He headed back toward a door to the right.

"Miss Martin," I shouted, "note that extension cord over there. Somebody could trip on it."

"Yes, Mr. Smith."

Lori scribbled away.

"And the fumes. We will need to check those MSDSes very carefully. A lot of VOCs." I turned to Ernie. "Where do you store your blanket wash?"

He clearly didn't know. He left us to talk to a pressman. I took the opportunity to whisper to Lori. I had to cup my hands and speak directly into her ear.

"We've found what we want. Now we've got to get out of here somehow. When we get to boss man's office, pour on the charm."

"I'll try but this suit doesn't make it easy," Lori screamed into my ear.

It made no sense to whisper. Nobody could hear a word we said three feet away.

"You'll find a way."

"What's VOCs?"

"Volatile Organic Chemicals. That's what you're smelling. They're bad for the environment and can cause cancer. Plants like this are regulated as to the percentage that can be released into the air."

"You learned that from Howie?"

"Yes."

Ernie had returned.

"The blanket wash is kept over there."

He gestured toward a yellow cabinet by the wall. We walked over to it. The cabinet contained several fifty-gallon drums of blanket wash. Howie had told me the stuff was just like gasoline and very flammable.

"You know these barrels should be grounded."

"Grounded?"

"Yes, that's regulation. A spark from static electricity could blow up this whole place. Note that Miss Martin."

"I've got it." She smiled at the gruff man and patted him on the arm. "Mr. Smith is just doing his job. Nothing personal. I'm sure you understand. But the law is the law."

I thought Lori had struck a good note to get us out of there. I let Ernie know the inspection was finished. He let go a sigh of relief and guided us back to his boss's office.

"I'm Anthony Imperiale, General Manager. How can I be sure you two are who you say you are?"

We sat in a massive office with windows looking out over an endless stretch of desert. Hazy mountains in the distant background. It was furnished in faux Western style, cowboy paintings on the wall, Navaho rugs, potted cacti, and an elk head staring down from behind his desk. The ambiance fitted Nevada but he didn't. His suave voice had an Eastern intonation. I handed him one of my cards.

"Call this number."

He dialed, talked on the phone for a few minutes, and was satisfied. The number was the office phone at Big Emma's. Lori's brother Joe was on the other end.

"I am sure we can work something out here, Mr. Smith and Miss Martin." Lori gave him her biggest smile, crossed her legs and pulled up the skirt of her suit, exposing as much leg as possible. "I would be happy not to get sidetracked by a lot of paperwork over some minor infractions. And I'd be most grateful for anything you can do to help me in that respect. I always find a way to express my gratitude."

"I'm sure that you're not offering us a bribe, Mr. Imperiale, as that would be a federal felony offense."

"Of course not."

"We will have to make our report. You will get a letter from my office outlining the areas that are in violation of the law. Then we will schedule a return inspection. If these areas are cleared up, and if you have no history of prior violations, there are unlikely to be any fines."

"There have been no priors. We're a new plant."

"Mr. Smith."

Lori looked at me.

"Yes?"

"We do have a tight schedule this afternoon."

"Right you are."

Lori rose from her seat and walked over to Imperiale's desk before he had a chance to rise. She squeezed his hand.

"It's been a pleasure, sir. Thank you for your cooperation. We'll find our way out."

She abruptly turned and headed toward the door. His eyes followed her swinging derriere.

I walked swiftly after her, holding tightly to my briefcase. She opened the door and we almost collided with Ernie. We rushed passed him and headed toward the outer plant door. Once again the redhead dashed out from behind her desk. I was afraid she was going to trip in her cowboy boots. At the same time Imperiale joined Ernie by the door to his office. I smiled blandly into their blank faces, turned and walked out.

The blazingly hot sun smacked me in the face. Hell couldn't be much worse. I looked back as the glass outer door closed behind us. Imperiale stared at my satchel. Then he whispered into Ernie's ear. Ernie took a walkie-talkie out of his pocket and began speaking into it.

I clutched the briefcase so tightly I could see the white of my knuckles. I turned and walked swiftly toward the car. Lori scurried after me. I wasn't concerned about appearances. Just wanted to get the hell out of there. Hopefully in one piece with the evidence.

21.

I started up the engine of my Taurus, jammed it into reverse, swerved around, and shifted into drive. I glanced in the rearview mirror. Imperiale grinned back at me. Reminded me of good old Red. Then he turned and spoke to Ernie who was still babbling away on his walkie-talkie. I looked toward the front gate. Closed, and the same two men stood beside it. The one who had been prepared to shoot us when we entered, rested his hand on the grip of his Colt. The other listened to someone on his walkie-talkie.

"What are you going to do if they don't open that damned gate?" Lori asked.

"Crash through it."

"Great."

I gunned the engine and headed straight for the gate. The two guards jumped out of the way. The one with the Colt raised the weapon and drew a bead on me. I held my breath, lowered my head and jammed my foot on the accelerator. My bumper banged against heavy steel mesh. The gate's wings flew wide open. It wasn't locked. I glanced through the rearview mirror at the guard with the Colt. He lowered the revolver. I let out my breath.

I turned the Taurus right toward Sparks, wanting to get as much distance as possible between us and that plant. A

No Time To Mourn

barricade blocked the road about fifty feet in front of us. A man, wearing a bright orange hardhat and vest, waved a Detour sign. He gestured for us to stop.

"Been a bad accident up ahead," he said. "You'll have to make a U-turn here. Proceed past the plant and take your first right, then right again and it'll take you into Sparks."

I glanced behind the barricade and down the road. Didn't see anything nearby. A slight rise in the road blocked a longer view. I made the U-turn and then barreled past the plant as fast as I could. I breathed easier, slowed down, and headed in the direction of the mountains.

"Glad to be out of there," Lori said. "You were cool, Jim."

"Didn't feel cool. And won't until we cross the border into California. This state's the mob's turf."

"What did you pick up from the floor?"

"Dig in my briefcase and see for yourself."

My satchel lay under her feet. She reached in and pulled out the magazine sections.

"Shit. These are disgusting, especially the kids. What kind of weirdos would want to look at such stuff?"

"Weirdos with a lot of money. There's porn and porn. This stuff is illegal to print or sell anywhere. They can ask any price they like for it."

"We live in a sick world. What happens to twist people so?"

"I'm not sure we know. Lots of time, though, there's some kind of sexual abuse in childhood. The guys who buy this stuff are mentally ill. Worse are the people like Imperiale. Out to make a fast buck off other peoples' sicknesses."

"Do you think Edward knows what's being printed out here?"

"Possibly. My sense is he's in over his head with the mob. They knew he was stealing from Color Graphics to pay for his gambling debts. That was their hold on him. Once they had him by the short hairs, whether he knew or not, he had no say. He warns Imperiale that Poppa is catching on to his schemes.

Tim Wohlforth

Imperiale hires Red to bump off Edward, Senior. Junior gets greedier. Together they work out the Enterprise Printing scheme. Susan begins to catch on. Imperiale brings Red back to finish off Susan. He couldn't afford to have anyone look at his relations with Edward and what was going on at this plant."

"And Red gets in touch with Edward. Gets him to make that phone call that set up Susan."

"Yes."

Still there was the photo business. Seemed to lose significance the more I learned about Edward and his mob friends. But it bothered me.

I drove in silence, absorbed by the peaceful mood of the empty desert. The driving was hypnotic. A straight-as-an-arrow black line of macadam as far as I could see. The road seemed to float upward over the horizon and on into the heavens.

I tried to digest our recent experience. I wanted to bust Imperiale's porno ring wide open, whether it was connected to Susan's murder or not. The problem was I had outsmarted myself. I had concocted a clever way of entering the plant by impersonating federal employees. Since I was a private citizen, not a police officer, the evidence I gathered was admissible in a court. However, I couldn't reveal it without exposing myself to prosecution over the impersonation gambit. I couldn't go running to the Nevada cops. Damn it. I now knew too much.

"Where's that detour?" Lori interrupted my thinking.

"Good question. I've been looking for a road to turn right on. Haven't been any roads that went either direction. People in Nevada have a different sense of distance. They drive fifty miles the way we hit the neighborhood convenience store."

I looked around us as I drove on. We were surrounded by a vast stretch of nothingness. We passed a deserted gas station and general store. The rusted gas pump was the kind with a glass cylinder that you filled by using a hand crank. A weathered sign announced the place as "Rawhide Canyon, Population 2." The two had long gone. Everywhere sand, rocks, gravel with the same monotonous tan hue. Here and there a scrawny dark green creosote bush. An occasional towering ocotillo, bent over precariously, sported an outlandish red flower as if defy the area's drabness. The mountains had taken on a deep red-purple cast. They seemed no closer than they had been back in Sparks. Not a single car had passed us since we left the plant.

"Why don't you check the map in the glove compartment?" I asked.

Lori pulled out a Nevada map and unfolded it.

"Fuck! Talk about detours! That guy's got us driving all the way to Pyramid Lake, then we turn right and go to a little town called Nixon, turn right again and drive maybe fifty miles to Wadsworth on I-80, then right to Sparks. I'd say it's at least one hundred miles."

"You've got to be kidding."

"No, I'm not. Stop the car and take a look for yourself."

I did as Lori suggested. I certainly wasn't worried about blocking traffic in that isolated spot. In fact nothing would cheer me up more than to see another human being.

She was, of course, right. We both agreed it would be ridiculous to continue. It made more sense to make a U-turn, risk going past the plant again, and hope they had cleared the road by the time we got closer to Sparks.

I got out of the car to look around, stepping into a hellish furnace. We wouldn't have lasted more than a few hours out there without water. The road had narrowed to a one-lane potholed macadam track. Insufficient room to safely make a U-turn. No shoulder. I didn't want to get stuck in sand in the middle of no place. I walked to the edge of the pavement and felt the sand with my foot. Soft.

I looked ahead and saw a dry wash about ten feet in front of us. A large culvert, designed to carry water from the wash, passed under the road. Hard to conceive of water flowing down that wash, but it did from time to time in winter and spring. I walked over to the culvert and found a turnoff on the other side. Possibly created by trucks unloading dirt bikes.

Bikers love to barrel along the washes. Good spot for us to turn around.

I heard a whirling sound coming from somewhere above me. I had searched in all directions but up for a sign of life. I looked into the sky. The burning sun blinded me. Then a black shape blocked out a portion of the sun. It grew bigger. A helicopter. Had to be the one that was on the tarmac beside the plant. I felt like a field mouse that had spotted a hawk in the sky. I had strayed too far from my hole.

I ran back to the Taurus, zigzagging as I went. The helicopter swooped toward me, the roar of its engines filling my ears, wind from its blades throwing dust in my face.

I glanced back. A man stuck his head out the window. He held an automatic weapon. An Uzi. An ear-splitting rat-a-tat-tat. A spray of bullets hit the ground behind me. I dived into the car.

"What do we do now?" Lori asked.

Eyes wide open, she grabbed me and pressed herself against me. I didn't answer because I wasn't sure myself. I gently pushed her away. I grabbed my gun from out of my shoulder holster and released the safety.

Another spray of bullets. One smashed into our back window. Glass shattered over us. Lori screamed. Little spots of red formed in her hair and began to spread. She brushed shards out of her platinum blond hair, her hand covered with blood.

I opened my window and, holding my gun with two hands, took careful aim at the helicopter. The huge bird swooped toward us, coming within feet of the car. I let go three shots in a row. One hit the copter's windshield. The chopper pulled up at the last minute, runners just missing the roof of our car.

I reached across Lori's quivering body, opened the glove compartment, and took out a box of cartridges.

"Let's go," I shouted.

No Time To Mourn

I dragged her out of the car with me and, weaving as I ran, dashed toward the culvert. I battled the soft sand, pushing too damned slowly ahead. Sand splayed around us. I felt like I was swimming against the current in a mad river. The helicopter circled around and headed directly at us again. I reached the wash, gasping for air, side aching. Lori's face was pumped red with excitement. Terror in her eyes.

The gunner let off another volley. The roar of the copter, combined with the sound of the Uzi, deafened me. Bullets plowed into the sand next to my feet. The bullets hit closer. The bastard's aim was improving.

I pushed Lori into the culvert, dragging myself after her. She pressed her trembling body against mine. We were both coated with sand and drenched in sweat. Lori's blond hair now covered with matted dark red blotches. But, for the moment we were safe.

"You okay?" I asked.

"Just scratches." Her turn to play heroine. "Now what?"

"Didn't you ask me that already?"

She smiled and gave me a big kiss on the mouth.

"You're the best there is. You saved us."

"To tell you the truth, I'm not sure what we're going to do. For the moment they can't get at us in here. I've got my gun and a box of bullets. We can hold them off, but not forever."

"I'm sure help is coming."

"I'm not. I haven't seen a car since we left the plant."

"Jim, there's something I've got to tell you."

"What? You've got to pee?"

"Seriously. I..."

The whirling sound of the helicopter grew louder and drowned out her words. Wind swept sand in on us. The machine was landing down the wash a bit. I was afraid of that. Positioning myself by the entrance to the culvert, I reloaded my gun. I gestured for Lori to lie flat on the sand at the bottom of the culvert.

"Jim..."

"Later. You watch to be sure they don't come around the other side."

She turned and faced the other end of the culvert. My worst fear was an attack from both ends. I could hold off the guy with the Uzi but what if there was another one with a gun? He could cross the road and approach the culvert from the other entrance. We would be like a fox at the end of the hunt, surrounded by snarling hounds.

I spotted the man with the Uzi walking down the wash toward us. A huge fellow with ill-kempt, shoulder-length shaggy hair, plaid shirt, jeans, and cowboy boots. It wasn't Red. Small consolation. I crouched down to my best shooting position and, holding the gun in my two hands, I raised the barrel to eye level. I had his chest right in my sights. I let off a volley of three shots. One bullet hit his arm just as he fired a round of bullets. They were way off the mark. He retreated down the wash toward the helicopter, holding his bleeding shoulder in his hand.

"That's one for the good guys," I shouted to Lori.

"Clint Eastwood, *Dirty Harry?*"

"That was 'Make my day.' We're okay for the moment, but my guess is he'll bandage himself up and return. They've got all day."

"Optimist. Jim..."

A new sound echoed through the culvert. Louder than a heavy metal concert. Like Field Marshal Rommel, the Desert Fox, had shown up with a whole Nazi Panzer Division of tanks. Certainly the terrain for it.

The roar of the helicopter's rotors joined the cacophony. Wind swept sand through the culvert and into my eyes, blinding me. The helicopter rose from the ground and then became nothing more sinister than a spot in the sky.

22.

Lori ran out of the culvert and started waving.

"Well, it's about time," she shouted.

I scrambled out after her and up onto the pavement. I found myself surrounded by the members of the Devil's Dykes Motorcycle Club. Lori made the rounds, giving each of them a kiss and a hug. Then they surrounded her, looking at her head wounds. Edith found a first aid kit and cleaned up the cuts. Lori's poor hair was now a complete mess.

The massive Mildred strode toward me, a smile on her face. She threw her arms around me and gave me a body hug that took my breath away. She was growing to like "Dickhead."

"Where'd you all come from?" I asked Mildred.

"Lori will explain. Our mission is to get you safely out of here before that helicopter returns."

I looked at Lori and asked, "Why didn't you tell me?"

"I tried to, Jim, but you kept cutting me off."

"Did you see a road accident somewhere between Sparks and the printing plant?" I asked Mildred.

"The road was completely clear."

I figured as much. Imperiale probably set up the detour scheme the second we walked into the plant. Kind of a back-up in case we weren't what we said we were. Then he saw me pick up those porno sheets and knew he had to act. What better way than to get us out in the middle of nowhere where the only witnesses were cacti and then attack us. He wanted the porno stuff back, and he didn't care who he had to kill to get it.

Lori freed herself from her biker friends and approached me, holding Edith by her hand.

"We're going up to the lake," Lori said, "and I'm riding on the back of Edith's Harley."

"We are? Don't you think we ought to get back to Sparks as quickly as possible?"

"No way can we pass that plant without an escort. They won't attack us with so many witnesses. And the girls have their heart set on camping."

"Camping?"

"You'll love it," Mildred said. "You don't think we cycled way out here just for you guys."

It's not like I had a choice. You don't argue with the Devil's Dykes, particularly Mildred.

The ladies returned to their bikes. The roar of engines almost burst my eardrums. I walked back to the Taurus, got in and started the engine. Lori, Edith, and Mildred were in charge. I was the tolerated guest.

I drove on toward the mountains. A blast of hot air rushed in the space created by my missing back window. I began to sweat despite the air conditioning. If there had been any witnesses to this strange procession, they would have seen a motorcade made up of one dusty bullet-ridden Taurus surrounded by a dozen large women on Harleys. The motorcycle riders would have been all dressed in leather except for one wearing a blue business suit with loose platinum blond hair trailing behind her.

After half an hour the road began to wind, rising up into desert hills spotted with mesquite and the occasional barrel

No Time To Mourn

cactus. Twisted Joshua trees sprouted at higher elevations. A rusted sign, riddled with bullet holes, announced that we were entering the Paiute Indian Reservation. Pyramid Lake came into view. Its sparkling deep blue water stretched for miles before us. Red and brown sandstone mountains rose from the right shore. The lake didn't seem real. So much water surrounded by some of the driest landscape in the nation. As if God had decided not to completely forsake this land and built His own private swimming pool.

We drove past the Indian town of Sutcliff. Nine miles later we came to an abandoned campground where cows grazed on what little grass survived in that environment. The pavement ended. We traveled on a dusty, bumpy dirt road for the next twenty or so miles along the lake's edge. As we approached the end of the lake, pyramid-shaped rocks jutted out of the shallow waters. I had read about this lake somewhere. Probably the *National Geographic*. Its pure waters came from the Truckee River, that carried snow melt from the High Sierras. My lady companions had decided to camp at the very end of Nevada's largest enclosed body of water.

Steam shot fifteen feet in the air out of a rusty pipe. Years ago someone had sought to tap the natural hot water jet. A stream of water so hot that it boiled as it ran down a little trench and into a large pool that overlooked the lake. Using motorcycle helmets, my lady friends and I toted water from the lake to cool it sufficiently to tolerate. After reducing the temperature to what I guessed was a tolerable 110°, we stripped off our clothes and climbed in.

One dozen lesbians, some rather bulky, Lori, and I sat naked in the pool, steam rising around us. I felt like the Sheik of Araby surrounded by his harem. Only the harem members were far more interested in each other than in their sheik. Had it been any different in ancient times?

Sandstone rock formations that gave the lake its name protruded from the water. The sun was setting. The mountains on the other side of the lake took on rich iridescent tones of orange, red, and purple.

Our chattering group grew still. A score of white pelicans flew by in perfect formation. The mountains' hue changed minute by minute while the sun became a dull ball of burnt red. The wind picked up, sending ripples through the reflection of the mountains on the lake's surface. I felt hands grasping my hands. I knew why the Indians considered that spot sacred. Those hills, that lake, we fourteen human beings were one. Gaia.

We skinny-dipped in the lake to cool off. Lori used the opportunity to wash her hair. Then Lori and I put our business suits back on. Had no choice, but we did look ridiculous. The ladies cooked up a great barbecue and shared it with us. We downed a couple of cases of beer. The air turned cool. Typical of night in the high desert. Two by two the ladies stumbled off to their private nooks among the rock formations.

Lori and I were left alone. We sat on a ledge overlooking the lake, holding hands. The moon had yet to rise. The sky was so bright from millions of stars that I could clearly see the outline of the distant mountains.

"Okay, Lori. How did Devil's Dykes end up on that deserted stretch of Pyramid Lake Road?"

"You complainin'?"

"No, but I'm damned curious."

"Edith and Mildred were in Big Emma's when you phoned me to make final arrangements. I mentioned the trip to them. They nearly fell off their stools. Pyramid Lake's the group's favorite camping site. Mildred expressed concern about our safety. Well, to be honest, about mine. They knew the Oakland cops would assume no responsibility once we left the city. She insisted on organizing a trip to the lake to coincide with ours. Made me promise to say nothing to you. She didn't know how you would feel about women watching over you."

"The truth is that I loved it."

I stood up and took Lori by the hand. We walked silently to where the sleeping bag Edith had lent us was stretched out on the soft sand. We shimmied into the bag. Lori grew silent. I wrapped the sleeping bag tightly around our bodies to keep out the coolness of the desert night. I could still smell the scent of the ribs in the crisp air. Lori's head, hair still slightly damp, lay on my arm. I felt her warm body pressing against mine. Then she grew limp. Lori had fallen asleep.

I couldn't sleep. Perversely, the closeness I felt with Lori at that moment led my mind back to the time so many years ago of our failed attempt to live together. It was as if I had to torture myself one more time to justify my insistence on keeping my distance from the one creature in the whole world I truly loved. My thoughts drifted to that day Lori walked out on me.

I lay on the unmade bed in our small apartment in the Rose Garden area of Oakland, watching Lori pack her things. The apartment was in the rear on the second floor with its own private entrance and a little porch looking out on the back lawn. Flower pots, filled with red chrysanthemums — Lori's idea — lined the railing. She had moved in two months earlier.

Her little head, with its long blond ponytail, bobbed up and down as she neatly placed her clothes in a large black suitcase that was sitting on top of the bureau. She was taking her time.

Any word would have stopped her from packing. I tried to speak but my mouth would not form a single syllable.

Tim Wohlforth

A curious thing had happened soon after she moved in. We stopped talking. Talking for Lori is like breathing. I knew she was suffocating. I was to blame.

Lori didn't look at me. She picked a black bra from out of the top drawer, folded it in half, and laid it on top of the bureau next to the valise. Then she repeated the procedure with a red bra, nestling it in the cup of the other one.

I understood why she was leaving, but that knowledge didn't empower me to act. I had climbed into my concrete pillbox, like the kind that once lined our shores to protect us from the Germans and Japanese. I was looking out at her through the slits. But she wasn't the enemy.

Lori reached into the second drawer, took a neat pile of white turtlenecks, smoothed them with her long bright red nails, and placed them in the suitcase.

I should have jumped out of bed, rushed to her, pressed her body to mine. I didn't move.

Did I really want her to move out? I wasn't sure. I didn't want her to leave, yet I did. I wished her to be with me but I needed to be apart. I longed for that life I had when I was alone. My own cocoon, the peace and tranquility that came from a solitary existence. When I was alone I felt...safe.

Lori walked to the closet. There was no bounce in those long shapely legs. She reached for her black mini-skirt, took it from its hanger, strode back to the suitcase, folded it carefully, and placed it next to the turtlenecks.

Her pace quickened. She threw in baby doll nighties, unopened packages of pantyhose, two sweaters, her pumps. She rushed into the bathroom. I heard her furiously heaving her makeup and toiletries into some sort of container. She strode out, holding a small, bulging, garbage bag. She drove it into the case, wedging it between bedclothes and skirt. There was a tear running down her cheek.

She snapped the lid shut on her suitcase. The click of the lock resounded through the tiny bedroom. It hit me like a bullet shot from a revolver.

"I'll come back for the rest," she muttered. "Love you."
"I love you, too. Always will. It's just..."
"I know."

Those were the most words we had spoken to each other in days. She grabbed the bag with her two hands, swung it off of the bureau and onto the floor. She picked it up in her right hand and stomped out of the room without even looking back. I heaved a sigh of relief.

I didn't see Lori for about a week. Then I went down to Jack London Square and sheepishly snuck into Big Emma's. She greeted me with a big smile. I swung onto a stool and she placed an Oban single malt in front of me.

"How's the hunting?" she asked.
"Just some insurance cases."
"Dullsville."
"How have you been?"
"Missed you."
"I-"

She pressed a perfectly manicured finger against my lips. She didn't want to hear it. Didn't want to go there. Never again. She stood on her toes, leaned over the bar, and placed a light kiss on my cheek.

I opened my eyes and looked over at Lori, my former lover, my friend, head still on my arm, sleeping like a little child, a smile on her lips. I knew a bit more about myself than I did then. My adopted mother had told me about my difficult birth mother. I had reason not to reveal my feelings to women. Not to get too close. I was hurt in the past and I could be hurt again. And experiencing three different mothers in three years didn't help. Knowledge of what made me feel as I did, didn't change those feelings. I felt the way I felt. I feared, if I gave Lori and me another chance, I'd react in exactly the same way. In the end everything in life was a trade off. I missed having a deeper relationship with Lori, but I liked my life just the way it was.

Tim Wohlforth

I noticed a couple of wrinkles around Lori's eyes. Otherwise she didn't look like she had aged a day since our break-up. A woman of crowds, noise, the city, television. So out of place lying there in the quiet desert.

In the distance the howl of a lone coyote. A flutter of wings. Bats. A gentle ripple in the black waters of the lake. Mallard ducks. I looked up into a cloudless sky filled with so many stars I wondered how there could be room for them all. Space had to be infinite. I could just make out Orion the Hunter in the sky above our sleeping bag. Surrounded by so many, many pinpricks of light, he stood alone, armed with club and sword, fighting his own individual war.

23.

I arrived back in the Bay Area exhausted. Not your usual overnighter at the gaming tables. I let Lori off at Big Emma's, parked the Taurus by the wharf, and headed back to my boat and home. A man sat in a car near the gate to my dock area. My shadow. I had called Nina when we reached the outskirts of the Bay Area. I wanted nothing more than to fall into the sack and go to sleep. But I had work to complete first.

I found a manila envelope in the drawer below the nav, took the porno material out of my briefcase, and placed it inside. Then I composed a letter to myself on my computer. Typing my address, I created a computer address label. I wanted everything to be untraceable.

It's not like the old days with mechanical typewriters. One ink jet printer is like another. Any idiosyncrasies are caused by the cartridge, not the machine. I replaced my cartridge just to be on the safe side. I sealed the envelope and headed off for a post office in another part of the city.

When I returned to the boat, I dug out the file folder I had created on Edward Henry's murder. The major stories came from the *Oakland Tribune*. The feature articles were written by a Constance Hernandez. I had never heard of her. It was about time we met. I called the *Trib* and asked for Miss Hernandez. She was tied up on another line but I waited. When I finally got through to her, I explained my interest in the Edward Henry murder. I told her I would like to meet with her and get her impressions.

"I reported it all in the paper," she responded curtly.

"It's never all in the paper. What I mean is your own personal take on it, on Susan in particular. Off the record, of course."

"Just a sec. You said your name was Jim Wolf? You're the guy who discovered Susan Henry's body. They just turned that one over to me for follow-up feature articles. Got you on my list to call. The cops are giving out dip shit. Let's make a deal. You tell me what you know about Susan's death in exchange for what I know on Edward's."

"Settled. How about Big Emma's on Jack London Square, 11 A.M. tomorrow?"

I was greeted by a curious Lori as I entered Big Emma's. She nodded in the direction of my favorite booth under the portrait of Big Emma, and winked. I sensed a slight resentment. Lori liked to think she encourages me to find female companionship. Almost like some male buddy. However, she's a bit of a control freak. She supplies the women and tries to engineer the whole relationship. Her attitude is a bit more cautious, bordering on jealousy, if I come up with someone on my own.

"There's a Miss Hernandez who has asked for you, Wolf," she said formally.

I smiled back, not about to let her know that my meeting that morning was a business matter.

Hernandez sat facing away from the door. I didn't get a full view of her until I walked past her and sat down at the booth. She had shoulder length dark brown hair, the kind that looks black except when light catches the highlights. A half-empty glass of latté sat in front of her.

"Glad to meet you, Miss Hernandez." I reached out. She grabbed my hand with soft fingers featuring burnt red nails. "I'm Jim Wolf. Most people call me Wolf."

"Connie will do for me." She had the bronze complexion of a mestiza. I guessed her age at thirty and, best of all, saw no wedding ring. "Now let's get down to business."

Lori came over purportedly to find out if I wanted something to drink. I ordered a latté, turned away from Lori, and gave Connie my warmest smile.

"I'm interested in your impressions of the Edward Henry murder."

"Oh, ladies first?"

"Okay, what do you want to know about the Susan Henry murder?"

"Everything. All the cops have told us is that the woman was murdered. Of course, we know the daughter's been arrested for theft."

I told her almost everything I knew. I held back only my recent trip to Nevada with Lori. As I talked she scribbled furiously in a yellow pad. I doubt if she missed a word.

"That's one hell of a story. Can I quote you on something? Like the murder suspect. This guy you call Red."

"No. I'm skating on thin ice with the cops as it is. For the record, I'm not investigating the Susan Henry murder. My interest in Red is strictly personal. I like living."

"Gotcha," she said. Her eyes, which matched the hair, looked playfully at me. She wore a brown business suit and a white silk blouse. "Outside of what he looks like, you've got *nada.*"

"Maybe it's a good thing he doesn't understand what little progress we've made. If he starts running scared, and I think that's why he tried to shoot us on the Alameda beach, he may make a mistake."

"So what do you want to know?" she asked.

"Who was responsible for Edward's death?"

"I thought you told me the cops know the answer to that one. It was this guy you call Red."

"I gather they thought at the time Susan hired him. I think they are still playing with that possibility. What do you think?"

"I covered the Edward Henry killing right from the start. I had a police scanner and picked up the first dispatch. Got to the scene maybe ten minutes after the cops. The woman was shattered. I found myself holding her in my arms as she cried. Hysterical really. It could've been an act, but Susan deserved an Academy Award if it was. I took to visiting her daily in her home. And not just to get information. I was concerned for her."

Connie's dark brown eyes opened wider as she talked. The delicate gold cross with filigree that hung on a chain around her neck pulsated as she breathed.

I blocked out the rising noise level around us as the bar filled up in anticipation of lunch. Lori came over with a plate of biscotti and two more lattés. We hadn't ordered anything. I didn't look up at her. Then she reluctantly returned to her post behind the bar.

"Is this woman who keeps plying us with biscotti and latté the Lori who was running around the beach at Alameda with you?"

"Yes. She's just a friend."

Why did I add that "friend" comment? Connie was having a definite affect on me.

"Didn't mean to pry," Connie said.

"What made you stop your visits with Susan?"

"The drinking. I couldn't get her to quit. I tried to convince her to try AA. I can't be around drunks. Reminds me of my father."

"Sounds like you had a grim childhood."

"Not really. He didn't drink all the time. It was just that, when he did drink, I didn't want to be around him. Now about Susan?"

"So, the short answer is you don't think she did it."

"Gut feeling, but what do I know?" She shrugged her shoulders.

"If we accept for the moment Susan's claim that Red was really aiming at her when Edward got in the way, what stopped him from then killing her as well?"

"Red's not a very lucky assassin. There was this gray-haired lady in a green Volvo. She spotted him and called the 911 operator. Red sees her and starts to shoot at her. Susan uses the diversion to run away and hide behind a tree."

"Why didn't Red search for her?"

"Had no time. The 911 operator gets part of the credit by sending out a call immediately, not even waiting for the lady to finish talking. There was a patrol car coming up Lakeshore Avenue right at that moment. Getting back to work after a break at Colonial Donuts. We're talking three, four blocks away. Must have arrived in seconds after the call. Red had to hightail it out of there."

"No lead on the driver of the Volvo?"

"*Nada*. Every other resident in that area seems to own a green Volvo. The others have Mercedes."

"And their kids play soccer."

"You got it."

Our eyes met. She smiled warmly at me.

"You're getting crumbs all over yourself," she said.

"The biscotti."

"Got to go to work."

"*Hasta la vega.*"

"No mangled Spanish." She laughed. "If you want to see me again, ask in English."

I could see I was going to have no competition from Howie, the king of Spanish mangling, for Connie's affections.

"I'd like to see you again."

"Business or pleasure?"

"Both."

"You've got my number."

Connie rose from her seat, her silk blouse stretching across her breasts, and wiggled out of the booth. She headed for the door, turned and smiled again, just before passing into Jack London Square. A ray of sunlight bounced off her hair, accenting its rich walnut color. Lori took in the whole scene. I thought she would burst as she rushed from behind the bar to my table for a full report. You'd think she had to pee.

The manila envelope arrived in my mail slot at the wharf office the next day. I called Nina and walked over to Big Emma's to meet her. Lori was opening the doors when I arrived. She wore jeans, her blue Harley shirt, and had a broom in her hand.

"Let me know if we don't open your office early enough for you in the morning," Lori said with a smile. "I'll see what I can do to adjust our hours to fit your needs."

"Much appreciated. Has Nina shown up yet?"

"I thought it might be Miss Hernandez again."

"Oh, Connie."

"So it's 'Connie' already."

"You want a complete report?"

"Heaven forbid."

"Just business." Why I said that I don't know. I should have said "It's none of your damned business." For someone who loves his privacy, I let Lori butt in far too often. The least I could do this time was tell her nothing.

"Sure," she said.

I touched the hand holding the broom. Figured I better switch the topic.

"Let me sweep out my own office."

"Done."

"Just one thing before Nina gets here."

No Time To Mourn

I told her about the envelope I was about to give Nina. I explained that it contained the porno material. We had to assume that her prints were on the material as well as mine. I planned to tell Nina I had shown the stuff to her. However, I could make no mention of our visit to the plant or even the helicopter attack on us because we had impersonated federal employees to gain entrance.

"But won't Imperiale say something?"

"Never. Once he places us in the plant, we can testify to finding the porno stuff there. He won't take that chance."

At that moment Nina walked up the sidewalk toward us. Sweat soaked through her pants. Blades of grass clung to the laces of her running shoes.

"Did you run all the way over here?" Lori asked.

"No, but I ran around Lake Merritt. Guess who ran with me?"

"Denzel Washington," Lori said.

"No, a white guy. Our new mayor. We talked during the whole three-mile jog. Wanted to know about women in the police department, my childhood in West Oakland, that sort of thing."

"Did he take you out for a bowl of brown rice and bean sprouts?" Lori queried.

"Actually he did suggest we get something to eat at his compound. Then a yoga session. But I told him I had an appointment. Now what's this all about, Wolf? This is supposed to be a day off for me."

We walked inside. Lori headed back toward the kitchen. Nina and I found our way to my "office" under Big Emma's painting.

"Sorry," I said, "but I didn't think this could wait."

I told her everything that Howie had told me about Edward Jr. and Enterprise Printing. As promised, I didn't mention his name.

Tim Wohlforth

"Jimmie, my boy, you are in a whole world of shit. Ollie is not going to like it. You're not supposed to be part of this investigation."

"I'm not investigating Susan's murder. Just trying to run down Red and save my ass."

"We knew about Color Graphics' credit problems but this Nevada plant business is news. You say you can't give me a name?"

"I promised my source. I'm sure you'll have no difficulty verifying what I've told you. The main guy at Enterprise is named Anthony Imperiale. My belief is he's fronting for the mob."

"Belief?"

"That's all it is. Just rumor. I suggest you check with the Nevada authorities. I bet they've got something on the guy."

"Anything else?"

"Yes. A package arrived in my mail this morning. It's really why I called you."

I slid the manila envelope over to her. I had ripped it open. She pulled out the magazine signatures, holding them by the edges so as to leave no prints. She shuddered and read the letter. It stated that the enclosed material was found on the floor of the Enterprise Printing plant and further asserted that Edward Henry, Jr. was a part owner of the plant. The letter concluded with the suggestion that Susan might have been in a position to expose Junior's connection with the porno business.

"Who do you think sent this smut to you? Edith?"

"Could be. It might even have been somebody who works for Junior. A lot of people saw me over at Color Graphics. Or maybe a member of Edith's motorcycle gang."

"Anybody else see this?"

"Lori."

"Why her?"

"Why not? She's in as deep as me, now that she can identify Red."

No Time To Mourn

"So you think the mob hired Red to kill Susan?"

"I think it's a possibility that should be checked out. It could be the reason you can't trace the car. Nevada registration. You're in a hell of a better position to look into the mob business than me."

"About time you realized that."

"Please, let me know what you find out. I promise to keep clear of Nevada in the meantime."

"Hey, isn't that where you two dudes went a couple of days ago?"

"Lori wanted to gamble."

"Right. They got an Indian casino that's closer."

"She likes the lights."

That night I curled up on my couch aboard the *Sea Wolf* planning to spend a pleasant and productive evening thinking about the case. Jordi Savall played Marias on the viola da gamba in the background. I had a feeling I was close to solving the mystery. While I didn't know the name, or for certain, the employer of Red, I knew what kind of gun he used and what he looked like. I had discovered Edward's mob connection. He and his pals were now my prime suspects.

I had to let Nina and the Nevada authorities take over that side of the investigation. They had greater resources than I did. Just as important, I didn't relish tracking down the mob in the alien territory of Reno. I'd be like a Californian trying to weather a North Dakota winter. A bit too vulnerable. However, I vowed to return to Reno and Sparks if Nina didn't turn anything up.

In a way I felt relieved. I now had the time to pursue a different track. Follow the clue of the photo as far as it would take me. This required me to simply put aside those pieces of the puzzle linked to Edward. The phone call, his financial troubles, the Imperiale connection, the porno printing. Then I had to pick up the one piece that didn't fit – Susan's photo.

Suppose Susan was correct when she told me that she and she alone was Red's target the day that her husband got shot. Then her death was rooted in her own past and had nothing to do with Edward's inheritance. The photo then became key to finding Red's boss. All the pieces of the puzzle would eventually fit together. But differently. Oh so differently.

I was determined to use this opportunity to think through the case afresh starting with the photo. I would assume that Susan had two pasts, the one in Chicago that she remembered, and an earlier one with the man in the army uniform. Her real father?

I had been drawn to Susan by a feeling stronger than reason. I pictured her sitting all alone on that bar stool, dressed in black, clutching her drink, wrestling with her personal nightmare. A kindred soul with a missing past. At least I had had a mother who filled in some of the blanks for me. Susan's mother was dead. All she possessed was a mysterious photo of her mother as a young woman, standing next to a man that Susan vaguely remembered. A man that decades later still frightened her, like my birth mother frightened me. Susan had used that picture to spark distant memories, memories she felt might save her life. She had learned too little too late. Had Susan's past returned to kill her? I planned to find out. One way or another I would damned well discover Red's employer as well as Red. Then I would avenge her death.

I hadn't taken her seriously. I had seen a drunken woman and that had prejudiced my judgment. Events had unfolded too fast. Everything pointed in the direction of Edward and then Imperiale. They were still my prime suspects. But, perhaps their connection to Red and the Henry killings was more complex, more convoluted that it had appeared on the surface. Once I discovered Susan's secret, I might also expose an unknown link to Imperiale and Junior.

No Time To Mourn

Most important, I was damned if I was going to sit around and wait for Red to find me and then kill me in the way and at the time of his choosing. I would be the hunter, not the hunted. I would find Red, drive him out from under his rock, and, if I had the opportunity, kill the bastard.

I was wasting time. I had to see that picture again. Everything now depended on my friends, the Galvises.

24.

Teresa Galvis greeted me with a warm smile as I entered Blowups that afternoon. Once again, I felt I was stepping back in time in that old-fashioned shop. The smell of developer and fixer was stronger this time.

"Joseph," she called out without turning around, "our detective friend has returned." Then she said to me, "I think we're going to be able to help you. Not everything but more than you had before you walked in here."

Joseph parted the curtains that covered the opening to the back. He held a large envelope in his thin wrinkled hands. He walked over to the counter, reached into the envelope, and laid out a series of prints. These included full eleven-by-fourteen-inch enlargements of the faces of Sara and the man who stood next to her, a blow up of the adobe structure, and a very fuzzy detail of the tag on the man's chest.

"I've identified the church," Teresa said proudly. "It's Mission San Juan Bautista. A very beautiful place. They still perform mass there every Sunday. And weddings, too. I have shots of that very tower. See."

She pulled out an album from behind the counter and turned to a section marked "Mission San Juan Bautista." She had around two dozen four-by-six-inch color photos of the building and its surrounding gardens. After giving me an overview, she returned to a page containing several shots of one side of the ancient building. The similarity with the tower in the photo of Sara was striking.

"Can you be absolutely sure?" I asked.

"Yes. While all California missions follow a similar architectural design, each is quite distinctive. Notice the bells, two large ones and a smaller one higher up, centered over the larger ones. Also the bell tower is on the right side of the church. The only one like that among the twenty-one missions on El Camino Real is in San Juan Bautista. I have photos of every mission in the chain, including the ones in Baja. If you'd like to check them?"

"I'll take your word for it. Where's San Juan Bautista?"

"Not too far from here, south of Gilroy, near Hollister."

Hollister? I had never been there but the name stirred a buried memory. My mind flashed back to the day I first met Susan in Big Emma's. As I left her in the bar, she muttered something I took to be "Holster." It could have been Hollister. She may have begun to piece together more of her past than she had been willing to tell me. I suspected the photo jarred her memory. Damn it, I had attributed her mumbling to drunken rantings.

I turned my attention to Sara. Joseph had done a fine job bringing out all the details. I had been struck, when I first studied her face, by its cool eerie beauty. Now I could see the eyes more clearly. Fear? No, that was not it. Determination blended with sadness. She was telling herself to make the best of it, to be strong enough to survive this loveless match.

Then I studied the man. He had a tough visage, possessive, unyielding. If he felt affection for Sara, he certainly was good at hiding it. I wondered why these two had married? The photo did have the feel of a wedding photo. Then a thought occurred to me. Suppose she was pregnant? I looked at the original again. She didn't show. A forced marriage due to pregnancy would fit the mood of the scene.

"I spent most of my time working on that name plate," Joseph said. "I've used a special high contrast paper. I tried some of the techniques we perfected for work on aerial photography. What you see here is the best I could produce."

I looked closely at the blowup and could make out nothing. My disappointment must have been written all over my face because Teresa intervened.

"Come on, Joseph, you're torturing the fellow. Show him what you really ended up with."

"I did show you the best I could do," Joseph continued, "but I got some help. My son, Emilio, is a computer wizard. He pooh-poohs all my chemical trays and enlargers as old fashioned. He only uses a digital camera and a scanner."

"Emilio worships you," Teresa said, turning to her husband. "It's just that he does what you do in a more modern way." She directed her attention back to me. "He's a computer engineer at Lawrence Livermore Labs. Works on super secret satellite photography as well as the stuff shot by the Hubble telescope."

"I was leading up to that, Teresa. You never give me time. I gave the original and my enlargements to Emilio. He worked it in for me one evening. This is what he came up with."

Joseph pulled a laser print out of the envelope. Letters on the name plate became visible. I could make out a "J" then nothing clear, an "h", followed by another blur. His first name was John. The first letter in his last name was "R." This was followed by a blur. Then two of the same or similar letters. They could have been "l" or "t" or possibly even "d." But it could have been a mix of two similar letters like an "lt." The last letter was obscure.

"That's fantastic, Joseph," I said. "We're finally getting someplace. Teresa has helped us with the location of their marriage ceremony. These blowups can be used to identify the pair. We know his first name was John and we have a relatively narrow range of possibilities for his last name. I can't thank you enough. Above and beyond, as they say."

No Time To Mourn

"He hasn't had so much fun in years," Teresa said. "Joseph, don't forget about the other blowup Emilio worked on."

"That was Teresa's idea," Joseph said. "You hadn't asked for it, so we won't charge you. It's just that my wife was so convinced this was a wedding photo that she had Emilio and me blowup her hand." He pulled out from his envelope a small laser print and showed it to me. "See?"

Teresa had been right. There was a wedding ring on her finger. But no engagement ring. It fitted with a quicky marriage.

"One more thing," Joseph added. "Emilio came up with this list of possible last names. It may not help much. The computer produced a couple hundred of them."

I thanked them again, paid them, stuffed the prints back in the white envelope and left. Handel's "Halleluiah" chorus roared through my head. I was getting there, damn it. Finally progress. I felt like rushing back into that photo shop and giving Teresa and Joseph big kisses.

My next task was to gather as much information as I could about Susan's past, using my computer data bases and the phone. It didn't take me long to discover the total lack of any record of Susan's birth. I checked, not only Cook County, but surrounding ones. I ran a credit check on her. The earliest report was in 1965 when she received her first credit card under the name "Susan Kranowsky." It listed her age as eighteen. She had a social security number. How she managed the feat without a birth certificate I wasn't sure. I got out my yellow pad and wrote down her birth date, March 15, 1947, as well as the SS number. I checked her records at the University of Illinois. These verified the birth date.

I then turned to the parents. I had learned the father's name, Herman, from her credit application. I had a complete

Tim Wohlforth

bio on him: Born in Chicago in 1926, served in the Army from 1943 to 1946, worked as a clerk, and then owned a small grocery store on Chicago's Southwest Side, good credit, died at the age of seventy-four in 1990. Sara Kranowsky does not show up on the radar screen until 1952. Herman requested a copy of his credit card issued with her name on it. Her age was listed as twenty-four. That meant she was nineteen when she gave birth to Susan. Herman listed her occupation as "housewife." I found no record of Sara ever having an SS number. Most interesting, there was also no record of her marriage to Herman in Cook County or surrounding counties. They could have flown off to Vegas and gotten married, but I wondered if they were married at all.

I decided to do some phone work. Using my disk containing every listed telephone number in the United States, I punched in "Kranowsky + Chicago" and got six numbers. It helped that the name was not very common and there were several variants in spelling it. "Krasnowski" was the most popular. I dialed the numbers one by one and hit pay dirt on the fourth try. A very old lady named Eva who claimed to be Herman's cousin.

This could clinch it, I thought. If only Eva will cooperate. Both her hearing and her English were not very good. She was shocked when she learned of Susan's death and promised to help me in any way she could. I have always been amazed at the willingness of most people to pour out vital information about friends and relatives over the phone. It was all a matter of the way I pronounced "private investigator." I cough in the middle of the "private" and enunciate clearly "investigator." Most people love to tell tales. They need only an excuse.

"Let me ask you a frank question, Eva. Were Herman and Sara ever married? I found no record of it." I could hear her sobbing on the phone.

"Nobody knew, except me. We close, Herman and me. He had no brothers or sisters. They lived like man and wife, devoted to each other and to Susan. Sara was a beautiful woman."

"Why didn't they marry and adopt Susan?"

"They couldn't. That's all he would say. We're Catholics so can't get divorced. That's how I figured."

"Do you know where she came from?"

"West. She was Italian. Only Polish in our neighborhood, but she was accepted. Everybody loved Herman, so they love Sara. She recently go to Heaven, you know."

Yes, I had definitely found the missing Sara and part of Susan's lost childhood. The swell from some passing boat rocked the *Sea Wolf*. Then the blast from the boat's horn.

"What's that noise?" Eva asked.

"I live on a boat," I answered. "I know about Sara's passing away. When did Sara and Susan get together with Herman?"

"1952. I remember year because that's when Herman opened his grocery store. Kielbasa, Perogi. I used to help out in store. Cooka' the Perogi. Susan was like a daughter. I never married."

"Do you know when Sara and Susan arrived in Chicago?"

"Not sure, but I got the feeling they not there long before meeting Herman. Wait a minute. Let me think. Sara did say something once. About how lonely she was in Chicago before meeting Herman. Had to work and take care of little Susan all by herself. 'Two years of hell,' she say."

"One other thing. What did Herman look like?"

"Short fella. Round head. A little stocky."

Kranowsky was definitely not the man in the photo, and Susan knew it.

"Do you think you could recognize Sara if I sent you a photograph of her taken shortly before she arrived in Chicago?"

"Pretty sure. No one look like her."

"I am going to fax a photo to someone in Chicago who works for me. He will show it to you within the hour."

"I try."

"Thanks, Eva. You've been a great help."

With Susan dead I might need Eva in order to conclusively identify the woman in the wedding photo as Sara. I faxed the photo to Ed Sutton, a PI I know with an office just off the Loop.

I sat down and made up a chronology based on what I had learned. Some of it was guesswork but I felt pretty confident with the results.

1946 – Sara marries John R... at Mission San Juan Bautista, California. This probably occurred in the fall if we are to assume she was pregnant with Susan at the time.

March 15, 1947 – Susan is born somewhere near San Juan Bautista.

1950 – Sara leaves California and arrives in Chicago. Susan is three years old.

1952 – Sara meets Herman Kranowsky, moves in with him, and takes his name. Susan is five years old. Sara and Herman never marry because she is not sure whether John divorced her or not. Even if he had, they're afraid they might be found out and have to give up Susan. They bring up Susan as their own child.

1983 – Susan moves to Oakland and teaches school.

2001 – Susan marries Edward Henry. First Edward is killed and then Susan.

If her murder was rooted in this past, then some event occurred recently that forced the killer to hunt her down and shoot her. The place to begin the search for the answer was Mission San Juan Bautista and environs. I would go there the next morning. But not alone.

25.
I picked up the phone and called a lovely brunette who knew Spanish, a useful language where we were heading.

"I was hoping you'd call," Connie said. "I tried to reach you but only got your machine."

"Been out of town. I'll tell you all about it when I see you."

"So we're going to see each other again?"

"I had a little trip in mind."

I told Connie about what I had learned about Susan.

"San Juan Bautista. My old stomping grounds."

"You come from there?"

"No, but not too far away. I'm from Salinas, me and John Steinbeck. I do have a relative who lives near the Mission. My real connection with that area was my first job right out of journalism school. It was on the *Hollister Democrat*, the daily paper."

"Fantastic. You'll be a great help. Be sure to bring a toothbrush or something. We may get stuck overnight."

"You sure this is strictly a business trip?"

"Not really."

"I'll be ready at 9 A.M., prepared for anything. Pick me up in front of my apartment."

Tim Wohlforth

She gave me her address in Emeryville. I was sure Monty guessed my spirits had improved. The giveaway was when I fed her two plump mice for supper.

The phone rang. It was Ed Sutton, the Chicago PI. We'd gotten a solid identification.

Connie and I stood in front of the bell tower that was attached to the right side of the main Mission building. The day was heating up and there was no wind. I was inappropriately dressed. Jeans, button-down tattersall shirt, blue blazer. My excuse was that I needed to look proper when going on interviews. And jeans and jacket is just about as proper as I get. Actually I wanted to look spiffy for Connie. Connie in short tailored tan skirt and white silk blouse looked both proper and cool. But it was her turf.

It had been a pleasant two-hour drive directly south of the Bay Area. We had gotten caught up in a small traffic jam coming into San Jose, but that was par for the course. I had placed Vivaldi's "Concerti Per Viola D'Amore" in the CD player. I didn't know how Connie would react to the classical music. Couldn't be any worse than Lori. She recognized Vivaldi. When I told her the title of the piece, she laughed at the "D'Amore." I guess I wasn't being that subtle.

I stared up at the gently curving lines of the tower with its modest cross on top. A red tiled roof extended down from the main building and abutted the tower. The deep green of yucca trees offset the cream color of the adobe. Four doves were sitting under the lower bells. They noticed us and took to flight, swooping over our heads.

"No doubt about it," I said. "Sara and John were married at this spot." I took the blowup of the tower out of the envelope I was carrying and showed it to her. "Two bells with a smaller bell on top."

No Time To Mourn

"You're right, of course," she said in a subdued tone. I had noticed a change in Connie from the moment we first entered the beautifully manicured grounds surrounding the Mission.

Connie grabbed my hand and towed me toward a sign just to the right of the tower. We read it quietly to ourselves. "Mission Cemetery. Buried in this sacred ground in unmarked graves are about 4300 Mission Indians, Spanish and Pioneer settlers." The first to be buried had been a little girl on April 23, 1798.

"Come."

She continued holding my hand as we walked over to the edge of the bluff where the Mission stood. Another plaque marked the route of El Camino Real that linked the chain of Missions running from north of the Bay Area all the way down to lower Baja California. A rich green agricultural valley filled with lettuce, tomatoes, cabbage, broccoli, and fruit trees stretched in front of us. In the distance, perhaps fifteen miles away, a mountain range, burnt brown, rose from the valley.

"If you want to understand me," she said, "you've come to the right place. The Jesuits created us out of the Indians they converted to Christianity. They taught us Spanish, then put us to work in valleys like this. Our job was to support the mission so the friars could carry on God's work."

"You sound bitter."

"Maybe I am. My people are still out there in those very same fields. See them." She pointed at clusters of agricultural workers, looking like ants, bent over the crops, laboring away.

"So much has changed since the days of the Spaniards, but in some ways nothing has changed."

"Do you think your people would have been better off living the simpler life they had before the Spanish arrived?"

"Yes. As that cemetery sign illustrates, thousands died in the process. But I wouldn't be me. My ancestors come from mixed Spanish and Indian parentage. After the Spanish left, we became Mexicans. Then the Americans took over."

"I like the result."

"So do I, actually. That's why I have such complicated feelings about our history. Let's go inside."

We entered a gift shop packed with crucifixes, plaster statues of Jesus, and saint medals. I had never seen so many religious symbols assembled in one place. I felt like an alien in an unknown world. I didn't even know what saint medal to ask for. A woman volunteer, with gray hair and wearing a flower-print dress, staffed the cash register. I went up to her.

"Do they still perform Mass here?"

"Every day," she said proudly.

"Weddings?"

"Of course."

"Baptisms?"

"All the sacraments."

"Do you keep records here?"

"I believe so, but you'd better check at the parish office with the Father."

We passed through a door and entered the church. Connie reached into her purse and withdrew a white lace scarf. She placed it over her head.

"Used to be my mother's and her mother's."

Hand-hewn timbers that dated back into the Eighteenth Century formed the ceiling. An Indian design painted in earth tones of red, brown, and ochre covered arched columns. The windows were simple square panes of alternating clear and amber colored glass. Candles flickered in the rear and a slight scent of incense floated through the air.

We went out a door in the back and left the dim cool interior of the church for the bright sun of the Mission's garden. The sun was high in the sky. It must have been 100°. Too hot for insects. I took off my jacket and threw it over my shoulder. Connie, without even a bead of sweat on her forehead, smiled laughingly at me.

In the distance I heard the hum of a mower. A brown-skinned man with a large sombrero mowed the lawn beyond the garden. The scent of freshly cut grass fused with the gentle

No Time To Mourn

aroma of blooming flowers. Yellow, orange, and pink roses, dark red fuchsia, purple bougainvillea blended together to create a breathtaking jumble of color. A palm tree, yuccas, a tall thin saguaro cactus, and the largest pear cactus I had ever seen, completed the picture.

"I'm not a practicing Catholic," Connie said, "and I learned in college about the dark side of the Mission system. But that place is special." She gestured toward the church. "People have gathered under those old beams for two hundred years, expressing their humility and their love. Each one of them, man, woman and little child, has impregnated those walls with their souls. I can feel it."

"It doesn't fit."

"What doesn't fit?"

"We came down here looking for evil."

"I see what you mean. We have followed the scent of a killer and here we are. Heaven on earth."

I put on my jacket, opened a door and stepped into the parish office. A Hispanic woman sat behind a counter. She had curly black hair, fine red lips, gold loops in her ears, and wore a tan business suit. She was around twenty-five. I could see her engagement ring and wedding band. In the sitting room to the right, a little girl, probably her daughter, watched TV. The receptionist was talking into a headset. After a minute or so, she turned and smiled at us.

"How can I help you?"

"We need some information," I said. "Are old records on marriages and baptisms kept here?"

"Only back as far as 1945. Anything earlier is stored by the Archdiocese in Monterey."

"We're interested in the years 1946 and 1947."

"Just one minute." She turned back to her phone console and pressed some buttons. She talked for a moment in a low voice. Then she faced us. "The Father says those records are not open to the public."

"Could we speak to the Father?" Connie asked.

"Of course."

A boyish-looking young man came out of an office just to the left of the reception area. Black short-sleeved cleric's shirt, stiff white collar, glasses, and light brown hair.

"How can I help you?" he asked. "I am the Reverend Timothy Cullman."

"Father, I'm Constance Hernandez and I'm a reporter with the *Oakland Tribune*." She handed him one of her cards. "This is Jim Wolf, a private investigator who is helping me out. We're looking into the murder of a woman who we believe was born near here and baptized in this church. Her mother was married here in 1946."

"You're not a relative?"

"No, but I'm from this area. Do you know Bennie Hernandez?"

"Yes. He lives down the road. Volunteers all the time to help keep up the grounds. Very devoted to the Mission and the Church."

"My Grand Uncle."

"Still, Miss Hernandez, we have a responsibility to our parishioners, even those who have departed, to maintain their records in confidence."

"That's what brings us here. A former parishioner has been brutally murdered. These records, over fifty years old, can help us discover who committed this evil act."

Connie's eyes widened, pleading with him for his understanding.

"If perhaps you could explain how these old records could be of any use?"

I told him the story of Susan's death and showed him Sara's wedding photo. I explained why it was we didn't know

No Time To Mourn

the last name of Sara's husband and therefore Susan's original name.

"That picture was definitely taken at this Mission," Father Cullman confirmed. "I've visited all the Missions along El Camino Real."

"We really would appreciate your help," Connie said.

"It's a mystery." He smiled. "I love mysteries, both heavenly and earthly."

"You can be part of the solution to this one," Connie suggested.

He seemed taken aback. As if Connie had sensed the youthful streak of adventure that was still in him.

"Why don't you two come with me?" he asked formally.

We walked down a hallway and entered a room filled with filing cabinets and old ledger-sized books with gold-stamped red-leather bindings. A phone sat on a desk at one end.

"This is not going to be easy," Reverend Cullman said in a tone that suggested that the challenge intrigued him. A boyish grin revealed his excitement. Day-to-day running of a mission had got to be a bit boring. Even in such a lovely setting.

"We don't have the last name," he continued. "Copies of all marriage certificates are filed in those cabinets by year and then alphabetically by last name." He indicated a row of filing cabinets at the end of the room. "It will take some time to check each one filed under 1946."

"We're pretty sure the wedding took place in the Fall," I said.

"I have an idea," Father Cullman said. "All wedding couples are asked to sign our roster as well as their certificates. They would be in there in chronological order. See those books with the red bindings."

He began to search through a pile of them that had been thrown haphazardly on a shelf. We joined the search.

"It's kind of a mess. We were going to microfilm these but didn't finish the project. We never seem to have enough funds."

"Here's 1946," Connie said.

She carried one of the volumes over to the desk. Cullman and I hovered over her as she turned the yellowed pages. She slowed down when she reached September dates. I pulled out the computer-enhanced laser print of the groom's name from the envelope I was carrying.

"Found him!" the priest exclaimed. "John Ratto. It's got to be the right one. See the name in the bride's space. 'Sara Agostino.'"

"Now that we have a last name," I said, "let's check the baptismal records for the year 1947."

The Reverend beat us to the file and feverishly fanned through the certificates. "Susan Ratto, correct?"

"Right," I said. "She was born on March 15th."

"Here it is. She was baptized in September."

"Wonderful."

"Could we have photocopies made of all this?" I asked.

"Just one minute." The priest turned to face Connie. "Could this be *the* John Ratto?"

"Possible," Connie answered.

He stiffened. His baby face aged twenty years in seconds. This priest was genuinely frightened.

"I'm afraid I can't help you. These records belong to the parish. I cannot permit them to be copied without first getting permission from the family involved. If I had only known…"

"Known what?"

"Never mind. What's done is done. I want you to leave this office immediately. I am sure you can find your own way out."

As we scurried out the door of the room, I saw him head for the phone on the desk. Then we passed the receptionist. A light blinked on her console.

"Who's John Ratto?" I asked her.

"He owns Hollister," she said without looking up.

No Time To Mourn

26.

I stood hyperventilating in front of the Parish office.

"Gotta get out of here."

Connie looked at me curiously.

"Why?"

"Suffocating."

I tore off my jacket and rushed down the path away from the Mission. She scampered next to me, trying to keep up. Sweat dripped down my brow. Salt stung my eyes. I reached my car and stopped for a moment in the shade of a large oak tree.

"You're serious. Too much religion?"

"Maybe. I don't know. It's like a closed-in world. I don't belong. At first I found the place enchanting. Now it's oppressive."

"I understand. When I was a little kid, it was just part of my life. Also the lives of my whole family. All my friends. Never realized how ingrown this very Catholic world really is. Then I went away to college. After that I couldn't return. I go to church from time to time. But really back? Never."

"What was going on in there? The change that came over that priest. Is this Ratto that powerful?"

"Yes."

"I thought men of God were supposed to fight evil."

Tim Wohlforth

"The Bible says 'Give unto Caesar...'"

"Is Ratto Caesar?"

"Yes."

Was that fear in Connie's face? She had struck me as the kind to stare down a paramilitary gunman in the Columbian jungle.

"You're serious," I said.

"Let Bennie explain."

She turned toward me and gave me a spontaneous hug.

We stopped at Doña Esther's Restaurant in the town of San Juan Bautista for some fajitas for lunch. Then I drove east on Route 156 toward Hollister.

"Turn left here," Connie said.

I headed down an unpaved dirt road toward an apricot grove. We were engulfed in dust.

"Stop. There's the driveway."

I would have driven right past and not seen the house. Buried among the trees on our left was a dirty-white square clapboard house. The roof came to a peak in the center. On old sofa, stuffing coming out in places, sat on the front porch. The windows and door opened to let in the breeze that didn't exist. A Fifties issue Buick stood on blocks in the front yard, no tires, rusting away. A Ford pick-up truck, not much newer but at least with tires, was in the driveway. We parked behind it. Chickens scampered freely in the front yard, pecking at the ground, stirring up dust. No grass.

I stepped into the heat. The shade of the trees helped little. Connie jumped out of her side and ran ahead, calling for her uncle. A large man with a barrel chest, a grisly white beard, and glasses, exited the door. He wore overalls but no shirt.

"*Niña.* It's about time you visited me."

"*Te queires. Como estas?*"

No Time To Mourn

"Bueno."

She ran up the steps and hugged him. Then she turned to me. "Meet my friend, Wolf. We were just up at the Mission. There's something you might be able to help us with."

"Come on in. Let me get you a drink."

We entered the dark living room. A garish tapestry of Jesus and the Disciples at the Last Supper covered one wall. A painting of Jesus on the Cross hung from the opposite wall. Blood dripped from the Crown of Thorns and from the nails piercing His body. Hot, fetid air smothered us.

"Be right back," Bennie said as he ducked into the kitchen.

A Lazy Boy recliner faced a small television set. Color images of a soap opera flashed through the room. The low drone of Spanish conversation drifted past my ears. An overstuffed couch, covered with white lace doilies, dominated the rest of the floor space.

I walked over to a glass-enclosed cabinet filled with clay folk sculptures from Mexico, its top covered with photos. I spotted one that looked like Connie as a teenager, with Bennie and an elderly woman in the background.

"Yes, that's me." Connie had walked over to my side. "The woman's my grandmother."

Bennie returned with a bottle of tequila, another bottle filled with a red liquid and labeled "Sangria," and six shot glasses. He settled in on the couch. Connie nestled next to him. I collapsed into the recliner. Too comfortable. I had to fight the urge to push back and fall asleep.

"I can't handle that stuff, Bennie," Connie said.

"Wolf will love it," he said.

He gave me a lesson in traditional tequila drinking. The idea was to toss down a shot of the clear tequila and then immediately follow it with a shot of the red liquid. No tame margaritas for Bennie. I gave it a sporting try. The Sangria was sickeningly sweet and hot at the same time.

Tim Wohlforth

Somehow the combination socked it to me. The heat of the room added to the effect. Connie might need to drive us on to Hollister. I felt so out of my element. I had been spooked by a church. Now I had entered the world of one of those specks in those fields below the Mission. Poor, warm, hospitable. The environment that had produced Connie. And Susan.

I left the first stage of questioning to Connie. I sank into the recliner, convinced I had been transported deep into the hinterland of Mexico.

"Tell Wolf about John Ratto, Uncle Bennie," Connie said.

"Which one?"

"There's two?" I asked. They ignored me.

"The father just passed away a few months ago," Bennie said. "His son now runs the business, 'John Ratto & Sons.' You saw all that land in the valley below the Mission? Most of it is either owned or leased by Ratto. I lease him the land around this house. Those are his apricot trees. Big man now. Huge tomato processing plant in Hollister. Virtually owns the town. The golf course. Housing subdivisions."

"Tell us about the old man first," Connie said.

"A tough guy. Used to have a little farm over Hollister way. I worked for him sometimes. Picked lettuce. I can pick anything. He never wanted to pay me. None of us had much in those days and some of us still don't have much."

"Do you remember his first wife?" Connie asked.

"*Muy bonita*. He treated her like dirt. Same with the daughter. I knew the midwife. A cousin. She told me about the birth of the child. Susan, I think her name was."

"Tell us," Connie said.

"John lived in a small weathered ranch house with a windmill, its vanes in tatters, situated on a dusty back road not far from here. It was summer and hellishly hot. John called my cousin, Maria. She rushed over to the place and found the wife, Sara, lying naked on an unmade four-poster bed, its sheets soggy with sweat. Flies circled in the air. Pain contorted her face, lovely red hair knotted, tangled. She was having a difficult delivery. Common with first births.

"John stayed out in the field, picking lettuce. Sara shrieked in pain as the baby came out. Maria called out to the field for John. He walked into the room. Maria told him the child was a girl. John winced at the word 'girl.' He turned his back on his wife in disgust. Without so much as offering a word of comfort he stomped out of the room. John return to his lettuce picking."

"Nice guy," I said.

"A lot like him in those days," Bennie said. "Best not be a woman."

"Let me show you something, Bennie." I took the blowup of the groom's face out of my envelope. "Recognize him?"

"That's John. No question about it."

"And her?" I showed him Sara's picture.

"That's Sara. His first wife. Just like I said, *muy bonita*.

"He remarried?" I asked.

"He got a special dispensation from the Church. He was smart second time around. That Sara came from a poor family. John was a big, good-looking man. Married into some money and property. They had the one son, John, Jr. I got to hand it to old John. He took what he got from his second marriage and multiplied it many times over. Wealth and power was all that interested him. Look at what he had when he passed away and what I got now. We both started out with *nada*."

"I'll take you, Bennie," Connie said, smiling and squeezing his arm.

"You always were a sweetheart."

Bennie turned toward me. "Want more tequila?"

"No thanks. Still recovering from the first shot."

He poured himself another combination.

"It takes practice, *amigo*."

"We better be heading off," I said. "We have a few questions to ask the surviving John Ratto."

I climbed out of the recliner with difficulty and wobbled toward the door. Connie gave Bennie a kiss on the cheek and joined me.

"Be careful, Wolf," Bennie said. "*Muy Cuidado.*" He rose from the couch.

"Why?" I asked, sensing fear in Bennie's voice.

"I said old John was tough and he was. But he was a straight shooter. Young John's different. Crooked as they come. Vicious."

"You have anything specific on him?" I asked.

"Take my word for it. *Peligroso.*"

I walked out of that little cottage as Connie received one last enormous hug from Bennie. I stood in the dust. An immense tiger cat pressed her dirty body against my leg. She paid the chickens no mind. Connie came to my side.

"That phone call the priest was making?" I asked, as I turned toward her.

"It was to John Ratto."

"You sure?"

"I would bet on it. That's the way things work down here."

"Sure you want to continue with this, Connie?"

"Wouldn't miss it for the world. It's about time the Rattos of this world learned they can't get away with murder."

She spoke confidently. Yet I sensed she knew much more about the danger we faced than she was telling me.

No Time To Mourn

27.
    I drove down a tree-lined street with small homes on both sides. The street widened, the trees faded away, and we found ourselves in deserted, blisteringly hot, downtown Hollister. Following Connie's instructions, I turned left on Sixth Street and discovered a parking place in front of a modern white single story building. A large sign with black gothic letters proclaimed it to be the home of the *Hollister Democrat*.
    I put fifty cents into the slot of a paper vending machine that stood in front of the building and abstracted the latest issue, a thin paper devoted to local issues. The headline that day: "Bar patrons still smoking despite law."
    Connie opened the door and led the way in. She asked the receptionist, an older lady, tall with dyed strawberry blond hair creating a tangle around her head, for Alex Brenner, the editor and her old boss.
    A tall, slim man, with flowing gray hair, came out to greet us. He wore a brown sports jacket with leather elbow patches, had intelligent blue eyes, and a warm smile on his neatly shaved face. I could smell an expensive men's cologne as he proceeded through a swinging gate in the front counter and came up to us. He gave Connie a light kiss on her cheek. She introduced me.

Tim Wohlforth

"What brings you back to the boondocks, Sweetie? Not enough murders in Oakland to keep you busy?"

"You guessed it, Alex," Connie said. "Actually it is an Oakland murder that concerns us. Its roots lie in Hollister."

"I would have thought the only roots we have here are those belonging to tomato plants and garlic."

We followed Alex through the business office into a large room containing six workstations. Two were occupied by young reporters hard at work on copy for tomorrow's edition. Not my idea of a newsroom. Of course, I got my idea from a combination of my mother's tales and that old *His Girl Friday* movie starring Cary Grant and Rosalind Russell. I figured my mom for Rosalind Russell. Therefore I expected clattering Underwood typewriters manned by whiskey-swilling, cigar-smoking, cursing reporters. They should be wearing felt hats, bow ties, white shirts with stripes, spanners. Certainly not jeans and loafers. He led us into his large office off the newsroom and closed the door.

"Now what is all this about?" he asked.

He found a seat behind a huge desk covered with papers. He gestured for us to take the couch by the side of the desk. I told him the full story of the murder of Susan Henry and the trail that had led us to Mission San Juan Bautista and Hollister. I showed him my photographs. He let out a long, low whistle and then spoke.

"You know as well as I do that this is Ratto's town," Alex said, turning to Connie. "You work either for him or with him. If neither, it's best to leave town. I want this story, Connie. The Hollister and San Juan Bautista end. I'm sick of just covering garden club proceedings and the high school football team. God knows if I still have the guts to print it. I'm settled in here. Family. Soccer practice. Church suppers. Lion's Club. That sort of thing. But damn it, I want the chance to make that decision."

"You got it," Connie said, "and we'll cover your ass. All we want is access to public records," Connie said. "Your old newspaper files. Anything you tell us in addition will be completely off the record."

"Fair enough."

"Let's start with old issues of your paper," I said.

"Follow me."

He led us out of his office, down the hall and into a small storage room. He opened a cabinet door, exposing one hundred years of bound volumes of the paper.

"We may be small but we have history," he said.

I pulled out the volume for 1950 and we followed him to a conference room. I opened the volume on the table in the middle of the room and started leafing through it. Connie and Alex peered over my shoulder.

"What are you looking for?" Alex asked.

"The story on the disappearance of Sara Ratto," I answered.

"Try March 15th or 16th," Connie suggested.

"Why?" I asked as I flipped the pages until I reached March papers.

"Just a hunch. That was the date Susan was born. Her three-year-old birthday might have triggered the mother."

Connie was right. The March 16, 1950 issue featured the story of Sara's and Susan's disappearance on the front page. All three of us read the account silently. John had spent March 15th in Gilroy, looking into farm business. When he returned home, he discovered his wife and daughter missing. The remains of a little birthday cake sat on the dining room table. Sara had taken two suitcases full of her and Susan's clothes. Also missing was Susan's favorite Raggedy Ann doll. The police reported no signs indicating kidnapping or foul play.

"I wonder if the bastard even bought a present for the daughter?" Connie asked bitterly.

"No mention of it in the paper," Alex commented.

I placed one of my cards at the top of the page as a marker and fanned through the bound volume again, looking for a follow-up story. Four days later another front-page story reported that John Ratto had filed a complaint with the District Attorney of San Benito County accusing his wife of kidnapping his daughter. The police reported that the agent at the Greyhound terminal remembered Sara buying a ticket for Los Angeles. They had taken the noon bus.

A photo of Ratto in his army uniform, a head shot of Sara, and a picture of little Susan, taken when she was two illustrated the story. Ratto wore the same stern expression as in his wedding picture. Sara looked younger than in her wedding photo and smiled confidently. My guess was a high school yearbook photo. Susan sported a sweet smile. The article also noted that Ratto had received the Purple Heart during World War II and participated in the local VFW chapter.

"It's clear where the paper's sympathies lie," Alex said. "Ratto being a veteran and all."

"Not to mention being a man," Connie added.

"Can we get copies of these stories?" I asked.

"Yes. Come with me. I'll drop the volume off out front and then let's go to my office. There's some things you need to know about Ratto."

"Old John Ratto was a big man around here," Alex began, feet propped up on his desk. "I've been watching his outfit grow for a decade now. Buying up land, then leasing more, taking over the tomato processing plant, extending his holdings into the Sacramento Valley, developing farmland east of here into a shopping mall, golf course, and housing subdivisions. But the son is even more ambitious."

"What do you mean?" Connie asked.

We had resumed our positions on the couch.

"Old John died about six months ago. Young John, as we call him even though he's forty-five, is involved in a merger with Genoa Lettuce, the biggest grower in the Salinas area.

No Time To Mourn

They have agreed to form a new company, Consolidated Produce. John is to be CEO and will control the majority of the stock. The merged company is valued at over a billion dollars and will be one of the biggest agro-businesses in the state."

"He had the resources to pull that off?" Connie asked. "I remember him as big, but not that big."

"You remembered right. He's put all his holdings into the deal and he's leveraged to his limit. But that wasn't enough. Remember what I'm telling you is strictly off the record. He's being bankrolled by people outside the area. They've sent in their own men to watch over things. That tomato processing plant of his is like an armed camp these days. Something smells, Connie."

"Like what specifically?" she asked.

"We heard this rumor about the new guards at the plant. A lot of the people who work there live in town. I sent a reporter over and they threw him off the property. So I call young John. Tells me the guards were required by the insurance company of the merger partner. Made sense. Then I got a call from McIntyre. You remember him, Connie, the paper's owner. Said to lay off Ratto. So I did. In a small town you do what you're told. Still, overkill. Made me more suspicious."

"Thanks, Alex." Connie beamed at him.

"As long as you're here, I suggest a walk down the street to the County Courthouse. The old man's will is still in Probate. Public records. Very interesting."

"You've been very helpful," I said, as Alex showed us out of his office.

"One more thing," he said in a very low voice, turning to Connie. "You got out of here. I'm stuck. As soon as you walk out that door, I'm calling Ratto. Telling him you are inquiring after him. Bet mine won't be the first phone call he gets."

"He's already heard from Father Cullman," Connie said.

"I wouldn't hang around this town for long. Or Cullman will be officiating at your funerals."

"You're serious?" Connie asked.

"Damned serious."

I picked up the copies in the front business area. The redheaded receptionist spoke into a phone as we walked by her desk. She looked up, stared at us with her icy eyes, and quickly hung up. I wondered if she got through to Ratto before Brenner.

The San Benito County Courthouse was a two-story white building with a porch around two sides. To reach the County Clerk, we had to walk up outside stairs and follow along an open roofed walkway to the Fifth Street side of the structure. The County was small and the staff friendly. They seemed pleased anybody was interested in the records they so meticulously filed. Within half an hour we had photocopies of John Ratto's will and related documents. Then I requested and received copies of Sara and John's wedding license as well as Susan's birth certificate.

As we left the County Clerk's counter with our material, I noticed a lady in the rear of the large room. A massive mound of flesh in a print dress, her face so layered with fat that no neck showed. She watched our every move as she talked on the phone. Ratto's agents were everywhere in this small town. I felt like a Soviet dissident in Stalin's time.

"Where to now?" I asked.

"The Boardroom."

"The what?"

"It's a bar just up the street on San Benito. Used to be a bank. We can get something to drink and sort things out."

No Time To Mourn

We entered a marbled, high-ceilinged room packed with the after-work crowd and found a quiet corner table. I took a seat, back up against the wall, my favorite position. I could see the busy bar, largely filled with men, and the tables of couples scattered over the room. A haze of smoke filled the air. The *Democrat* didn't have to stray far from its office to research its cover story. Connie sat opposite me.

Nobody waited on us. I got up and walked over to the bar. Sawdust covered the floor and a large buffalo head hung over the bar. The bartender had long sideburns and wore a Stetson hat and a fringed leather vest. Didn't blend with the bank decor. But what the hell did I know about old valley banks? I ordered an Oban single malt scotch. The bartender thought I was from Mars. I ended up with Johnny Walker Black Label and a Chardonnay for Connie. He waited on me silently. Conversation stopped around me. Then I carried the drinks over to my table.

We laid out the documents in front of us. John Ratto had chosen the Hollister branch of the Bank of America as the will's executor, not his son. That suggested he didn't fully trust him. The estate was to be divided evenly between the younger John and Susan. At least, in the end, John had wanted justice done for his daughter. That was to his credit. He had instructed the bank to make a "good faith" effort to find her. If she could not be located "within a reasonable timeframe," the entire estate then went to John. The total value of the estate had been established as three hundred million dollars.

Last week, the bank had submitted a report on its good faith effort to the probate judge. They had placed ads in the *Democrat*, as well as in the *San Francisco Chronicle* and in the *Los Angeles Times*. Their only other search effort was to run a skip trace on her. Since the bank used "Susan Ratto" for the trace, it turned up nothing. Not what I would consider much of a good faith effort, but this was Hollister and Ratto was probably their biggest customer. The bank requested that the judge release the entire estate to the son.

"It all makes brutal sense now," I said. "We're talking one hundred and fifty million at stake. We can rest assured that once the Young Ratto discovered the terms of his father's will he hired a private investigator to find Susan before the bank could. Then he hired Red to kill her."

"You're right," Connie said. "Without the whole estate, I doubt if Ratto, even with outside help, could have pulled off the merger. He couldn't count on the bank coming up empty-handed. If Susan had lived, she might have heard of the ads. She was already homing in on Hollister. John had to get Susan out of the way. What do we do now? Go to the cops?"

"With what? We can connect Ratto to Susan but not to Red. So we have nothing."

"Have a plan?"

She smiled. She knew I did.

"Tomorrow morning we visit Ratto and place all our evidence before him. We'll see how he reacts. My guess is he'll sic Red on me."

"You want Red to kill you?"

"I can identify Red so he needs to take me out. I don't feel like spending the rest of my life covering my back. So I force his move. I'm setting a trap. We catch him and we get Ratto."

"That's the best you can think up?"

"Ratto knows we're on to him already. The guy's stalking us. The priest, Brenner, one of his employees, someone at the courthouse, and now here."

"Here?"

"Don't look, but that bartender has been watching us for the past fifteen minutes. He keeps polishing the same glass. We're old news to Ratto."

"Frightening."

No Time To Mourn

I stood for a second on the empty wide sidewalk in front of the Boardroom with Connie at my side, trying to get my bearings. I felt like I had stepped into the oven of a bakery. Reminded me of the Nevada desert. Except concrete replaced cacti. The late afternoon sun, low in the sky, blinded me.

I heard salsa music. It grew louder. As if a band was marching up the street. A low rider with a sound system that could swamp Carnegie Hall lumbered toward us. Powder-blue, fin-tail Chevy. The front end suddenly rose three feet.

"Hydraulics," Connie said.

The car raced its engine, turned sharply right, and battered right up on the sidewalk. The front end dropped to within inches of the ground. The rear rose three feet. The bastards were preparing to scrape us up off the sidewalk. The vehicle accelerated and barreled at us. The salsa music blasted at my ears like a jackhammer breaking concrete.

I grabbed Connie's hand and pulled her with me back through the bar's door. We tumbled onto the floor. The low rider roared past, shaking the glasses on the counter behind the bar. Sawdust covered both of us from head to foot.

The bar's patrons turned away from the projection television set. They stared coldly at us. Pissed. We had interrupted their ESPN watching. The bartender grinned a crooked smile.

"Just some of the boys having fun," he said.

The crowd at the bar laughed. We had made their day.

"Friendly town," I answered.

28.

"Well, what do you make of that?" I asked Connie. We hustled out of the bar and down the sidewalk toward my car.

"Those were no 'boys.' I got a glance of them. Toughs. In their forties. They would have run us down if they could."

"Figure Ratto sent them after us?"

"He wouldn't have to. Half this town works directly or indirectly for him. By the time we hit the Boardroom most everybody knew we were in town and checking into Ratto. Maybe a couple of them just figured they'd do him a favor. He has many ways of repaying favors."

"Where to now?" I asked. "Too late in the day to find Ratto at his office."

"Let's get the hell out of this shitty town. I know a great restaurant in Gilroy. Good motel, too."

I liked the sound of that "good motel" line. Life was looking up. I vowed to drive Red, Ratto, and his hometown buddies out of my mind for a few hours and devote my attentions to the lovely creature next to me.

No Time To Mourn

We stood under the shower washing off sawdust, sweat, and grime from Bennie's farm. I took a bar of soap and a washcloth and massaged Connie's back. I kissed the nape of her neck. She turned toward me. I washed her face, neck, chest, legs. She returned the favor. We wrapped our arms around each other, pressing body to body, and allowed the gentle warm water to splash over us.

We stepped out onto a mat on the bathroom floor. I reached for two towels from the rack by the shower. I handed one to Connie and used the other to dry off her whole body. I patted her face, wiping off her forehead and cheeks and then her neck, kissing her neck. I moved slowly down her brown body, patting dry her breasts, arms, belly, each leg, the feet. Then it was Connie's turn to dry my body.

I held her by the hand and led her to the bed. She pulled down the covers and then stood beside the bed, smiling. Her delicate filigree cross dangled between her firm naked breasts. Nipples erect. She looked like a sculpture cast in bronze. For a moment neither of us moved. She smiled and held out a hand. I took it. She lowered herself onto the bed, drawing me to her.

We took our time.

I drove the Taurus into a large parking lot in front of the tomato processing plant. A sign on the side of the building proclaimed "John Ratto & Son Foods." It was ten o'clock in the morning. The sun was already blazingly hot. Connie squeezed my arm. I was tempted to turn the car around and head back to the motel in Gilroy. But I had a job to do. I climbed out of the car and stood in the hot sun. Connie joined me.

"Let's have a look around," I said, "before we go in to see Ratto."

We walked over to the left side of the plant where a semi had just backed in with two trailers filled with Roma tomatoes. A woman wearing a hard hat, blond hair splaying out from under the rim, and a bright orange jacket similar to those worn by CalTrans workers, stood on a platform next to the end of the last tomato trailer. She used a long pole with a hook to reach down and trip a latch on a trap door at the end of the trailer. Then she swung a pipe over the trailer and pulled a lever. Dirty yellow water blasted out over the tomatoes, forcing them out of the opening in the bottom and onto a conveyor belt. A continuous stream of tomatoes flowed up the belt to a level above the plant and then down into the building.

"Quite an operation," Connie said. "Certainly seems legit."

"There's something about the place that disturbs me."

"Like what?"

"Not sure."

"I'll talk with those drivers over there," Connie said. "Might learn something." Several trucks were lined up to unload. Their drivers stood around, chatting in Spanish. "Why don't you check out the rest of the plant?"

"Sounds like a plan."

The truck drivers stopped talking among themselves as Connie approached. They surrounded her, laughing and gabbing away. She was a pretty diversion from their workaday world.

I turned and walked along the front of the building. Wide open roll-up doors let in air. I suspected the temperature inside the building to be between 110° and 120°. Large No. 10 institutional-sized tin cans zipped along conveyor belts that crisscrossed at different levels and angles. Massive cookers spewed steam and heat into the air. A pipe pumped red fragments of tomato skins into a dumpster outside the plant.

The acidic smell of cooked tomatoes clung to the motionless air and stung my eyes. A Chicano worker sat on a forklift next to the dumpster. He had a handkerchief wrapped around his head, topped off with an orange hard hat. He

No Time To Mourn

carefully sprinkled salsa from a thin bottle onto his taco. You would have thought he had had enough of tomato products.

The place seemed ordinary enough, yet I sensed that I was being watched. After all those phone calls and that low rider attack, I was ready for anything. This was Ratto's town and Ratto's plant. Our friend Alex of the *Hollister Democrat* couldn't help us. He had too much to lose. I wanted to get the hell out of there. Yet, I sensed Red was near. I had to set the trap.

I looked up toward the roof of the building. A series of small TV surveillance cameras had been mounted at twenty-foot intervals. Seemed a bit much for a plant that produced tomatoes. Who's going to steal a bottle of catsup?

As I walked, the camera above me swiveled, keeping me in view. I quickened my pace. The camera turned faster. I stopped. It stopped. They knew I was there.

A man walked toward me. He was large and, despite the heat, dressed in a three-piece, navy-blue business suit, white shirt and red tie. He wore an orange hard hat and had a headset wrapped around his ear. A bulge showed under the jacket. I knew muscle when I saw it.

It was time I gathered up Connie and we hoofed it to the office. I circled back past another dumpster being filled with a mash of tomato waste and returned to the unloading platform. Another man, a Hispanic dressed in a white coat, the kind doctors wore, approached Connie. She handed him her card. The truck drivers melted back toward their trucks.

"You are trespassing, Miss. This is a secure area," white-jacket said. He spoke formally, without even a trace of an accent. Like a cop giving a speeding ticket to a Jaguar driver.

"I didn't know this was a defense facility. Looked more like a food processing plant." Connie sounded pissed.

"Funny," three-piece-suit said, as if he was commenting on a Jay Leno joke. He had come up to us from behind me. These were no ordinary thugs. Must have gone to a finishing school for hoods.

Tim Wohlforth

I saw no sense letting matters get out of hand. I walked up to them and asked, "Could you direct us to the office? We're looking for John Ratto."

"Down there in the middle of the plant, through those glass doors," white-jacket said.

"We'll show you the way," three-piece-suit added.

He talked in a low voice into his headset. I felt a heavy hand grab hold of my arm. White-jacket latched onto Connie.

"Hey," Connie said. "That's not necessary."

"Wouldn't want you to stumble," the guard said politely.

Connie whispered in my ear, "The guy in white was driving the low rider."

"Great."

We were escorted, more like marched, into the company office.

John Ratto sat behind a polished mahogany desk in his spacious air-conditioned office. We settled into two comfortable chairs in front of him. I turned and saw the outlines of the two security guards through the translucent glass of the office door.

"Now what is this all about?" he asked. "My secretary says it has something to do with Dad's estate."

"You sent two goons in a low rider to run us down yesterday afternoon," Connie said. "One of them is that guy right out there in a white coat."

"Who are you?"

"Constance Hernandez from the *Oakland Tribune*."

"Didn't you used to work down at the *Democrat*?"

"Yes."

"This town not big enough for you?"

"You didn't answer my question."

No Time To Mourn

"I don't 'send' people, Miss Hernandez. I don't need to. The people in Hollister just don't like troublemakers. I can't blame them."

I looked over the room as Connie and Ratto exchanged shots. It was completely sealed off from the noise and smell of the plant and pleasantly cooled by air conditioning. Association membership plaques, commendations of various sorts, and photos of the elder Ratto shaking hands with Governor Williams and Senator Feldman covered the wall behind his desk. A large silver-framed picture of the father from his mature years sat on the desk. The resemblance with the young soldier in my photo was striking.

Young John, like his father, had a rectangular rugged chiseled face and powerful barrel build. He wore a short-sleeved white shirt and no tie. Dark curly hair protruded through the open collar area. The eyes were different, however. The old man's were cold as an Alaskan glacier. The son's eyes burned with hatred. His body was tense. It was as if he had to exert all the self-control he could muster to keep from jumping over the desk and attempting to throttle us.

Ratto was my third bad guy in less than a week. Junior displayed a weak character, ready to panic at any moment, vicious but ineffective. Imperiale was murderously cool, in charge of his emotions, if he had any, used to commanding respect. Ratto had inherited a powerful presence from his father. It was as if boiling tomato product from his plant, rather than his father's ice water, coursed through his veins. Good. I wanted to infuriate him. To force him to act without thought. Looked like that was going to be easy.

"I have some photos to show you," I said.

"And who are you?" he growled.

"Jim Wolf. A private investigator hired to protect your now deceased half-sister."

"Not very good at your job."

I drew the blowup of his father's face out of the envelope I carried. "This your father?"

"Couldn't say."

"It comes from a photo taken at the time of his first marriage."

I showed him a copy of the original shot.

"Don't recognize the woman. Where'd you get this?"

"The woman's your father's first wife. The photo was given to me by your half-sister, Susan Henry."

He knew I had found something that connected Susan's murder to him. Why else would I be in Hollister asking the questions I was asking. He just didn't know what I had found. He had not expected hard evidence like that picture.

For a brief moment he let his mask drop. Behind the tough guy pose sat a frightened little boy. A boy who had everything given to him by Poppa. But Poppa was now dead and he was on his own.

He recovered and blustered on, "So you claim this Susan is my half-sister?"

"That's about it."

"You've got shit. Maybe that's just some old girlfriend of Dad's."

"In front of Mission San Juan Bautista? I have more. I have seen in a photo of Sara an old edition of the local paper, your father's first wife. There's no question that she's the same as this lady clinging to your father's arm. I have a woman in Chicago who has identified the woman in this photo as the Sara who came to live with Herman Kranowsky, to adopt his name, and to raise Susan as his daughter. I looked up your father's will at the courthouse and know that he intended half the estate to pass to Susan, if she could be found."

"Get the hell out of here."

If the guy got any more pissed, he'd burst and smother us in tomato paste.

"It struck me that the one person in the whole world with the most to gain from Susan's death is you."

"Both of you. Out. Now."

No Time To Mourn

He clenched his fist and rose from his desk. A big bastard. All muscle.

"Do you know a fat man who drives a red Saab?"

He rushed from around the desk, came up to me, and shook his hairy fists in my face. I raised my hands to defend myself. He pulled back his right hand ready to slug me. Then he grew limp and reached for the phone.

"I'm calling Security."

The kind of guy who liked others to do his dirty work. Like Red.

"Who's running this place, Ratto?" I asked. "You or those two guys out there?"

We didn't wait for an answer. Connie and I got up and headed out of his office. The guards blocked our way. Three-piece-suit pulled a .45 from out of a shoulder holster. White-jacket moved toward Connie. He stopped, staring beyond us. I turned to see Ratto gesturing to them to let us through. Not an appropriate place for another murder.

Three-piece-suit lowered his gun. White-jacket moved aside. We pushed past them and out into the blazing sun. The heavies followed us to the office door. They stood watching us as we walked out into the parking lot.

Connie gripped my arm tightly. The acrid odor of tomatoes filled the air. The parking lot was deserted. At a distance a truck, pulling two large open trailers loaded with tomatoes, drove through the gate.

I headed toward my Taurus, almost breaking into a trot. I had set the bait. Ratto was panicking. He may have hesitated from shooting us in his office. But out here? And did he control his partners and their agents? I had to get Connie out of there safely.

I heard the roar of a car's engine. Wheels spun on the loose gravel that covered the macadam. I turned. The red Saab swung out from behind the plant. I had sensed he was nearby. But not this close. Red raced the car's engine. He headed straight for us like a maddened bull, bleeding from javelin thrusts.

29.

I grabbed Connie's hand and, pulling her after me, ran zigzagging toward the car. The Saab turned as we turned. The Taurus was only a few feet away. Red gained by the second. The roar of his engine deafened me. I could almost feel his goddamn breath on my neck. He had to swerve. Had to. Otherwise he'd not only hit us but crash into the Taurus. Well, if we got it, so would he.

I yanked Connie to the right. We both smashed into the front of the Taurus. We fell to the ground and squeezed under the car. The Saab skidded, spraying us with gravel. The Saab careened past the Taurus, denting my fender.

"Gotta make it into the car," I yelled and crawled out from under the Taurus. Gravel clung to me. I turned to help Connie to her feet. Dirt covered her. Blood dripped from a scrape on her right knee. Spotted Red. He had headed out into the field next to the parking lot.

"Don't worry about me," she said. "That bastard's going to turn. We can't give him another run at us."

I unlocked my side, threw myself in. I reached over to unlock her side. She jumped in while I started the engine. Connie was wrong. Red was in the middle of the field now. Instead of turning back, he banged forward toward the macadam road. I shifted into gear and took off after him. I bounced over rows of dirt that once held garlic plants, spewing dust out in all directions. It was like I was driving on a washboard. Each bump shot through my spine like a sledgehammer. Not recommended for people with back problems.

"This is a reversal of roles," Connie said, smiling at me, as she clung to her seat. She hadn't had time to buckle up. "Now we're chasing him."

"And we're not going to let him get away. Sorry for getting you into this."

"Great newspaper copy."

Red reached the road before us. He turned left and headed toward Route 101. I knew, once he hit the highway, I wouldn't have much chance catching him in the traffic. He'd make it to San Jose and escape.

Once again Red surprised me. Barely slowing, he turned sharply right and roared down a country road. I followed suit. Within minutes we left all signs of life behind us. The road ahead went straight into the horizon. Heat waves rose from the pavement. It reminded me of Pyramid Lake Road. Only this one bored through farmland, not desert.

Acres of tomato plants lined both sides of the road. No one worked the fields. The Saab, a far more powerful car than mine, grew smaller. It became a red dot on the horizon.

"Looks like we're losing 'em," I said to Connie.

"What do you plan to do if you catch up?"

"Try to stop him."

"Then what?"

"Take him."

"He's armed."

"He carries a Ruger .22. Great gun for assassinations but no match for my .38 in a showdown. He won't get close enough to hit me."

"Shoot him dead? Just like that."

"Just like that."

"This is a new side of you."

"I've been preyed upon by that monster for too long. He murdered Edward and Susan Henry. He tried to kill me. I'm sick of being the hunted. Now I'm the hunter."

"You don't like getting sand kicked in your face."

"A bit more than sand."

"I understand. You're right, I'm sure. Just that I couldn't do it."

"No one's asking you to."

"Hey, he's slowing down."

Connie was right. The red dot grew in size until it turned into a car. He wanted us to catch up to him.

"It looks like you're going to get your chance." She frowned.

"Don't worry. You'll be safe enough. Just stay in the car on the floor."

"I'm not worried about myself. Don't want to lose you when we're just getting acquainted."

I smiled at her. The Saab sat by the side of the road. Tomato plants gave way to apricot trees. I stopped my car about fifty yards behind Red. No traffic. No houses. Even from the air, the two cars couldn't have been seen. I reached over and took my .38 and box of bullets out of the glove compartment. Connie involuntarily cringed as I drew the weapon past her front. I placed the bullets in my pocket and took the safety off the Smith & Wesson. Red made no move. He sat in his car, waiting for me.

I inched open my door, got out of the car, and crouched. Sweat dripped down my face. I peered around the door's edge at Red. Still no movement. It was now up to me. If I walked toward the Saab I was a sitting duck. I turned, and using the open door as a shield, I crawled to the back of the car. I made the mistake of touching the Taurus. It burned my fingers.

I dashed for the line of apricot trees. No shots. I tried to spot Red. The sun shown directly into my eyes. I ran to the next tree. Unfortunately apricot trees have damnably narrow trunks, but they offered some protection. They were spaced

No Time To Mourn

about ten feet apart. I shifted from tree to tree making slow progress toward the Saab.

I was about thirty feet away, when I thought I saw movement in the Saab. I shielded my eyes from the sun. Red's head protruded from the window. The sun reflected on a metal object. Red's Ruger, with scope attached. He raised the gun to eye level and took careful aim. I pointed my .38 at him, trying to keep the bulk of my body behind the tree. I had the killing power and accuracy advantage at that distance.

He fired first. Two shots. Pings again. Missed me. I fired, but he had ducked back into the Saab. He shifted into gear. Gravel sprayed from spinning wheels as he bolted toward the tar road. I dashed out from the row of trees, crouched into shooting position, steadying the gun with two hands, and let off a volley of three shots at the Saab. His rear window shattered. He kept on speeding down the highway. I turned and started to run toward the Taurus.

"Shit!" I cried out.

Connie opened the door on her side and came running toward me, throwing her arms around me.

"You okay?"

"He wasn't aiming at me. Look at my tires. Smart bastard."

He had taken careful aim and punctured both of my back tires. We were stuck. He knew better than to have a shoot out with me when I had the firepower. That wasn't his style. He liked to surprise his prey and then let off the single shot to the head.

"What do we do now?" Connie asked.

"Let's go back to the car. It's hot as hell out here. Then we call AAA on my cell phone and wait."

We climbed into the Taurus and I made the call. Luckily we had left the motor running and the air conditioning on.

"What about Red?" Connie asked.

"He won't bother us now. He'll head back to his lair, lick his wounds, and plot a way to get me. That's when I'll get him."

"You're confident."

"This is the end game. I'm getting to know this chap, how he thinks, what he'll do. I'll be ready for him next time."

"So we just sit here?"

"Not quite."

I pulled her over and kissed her. She pressed her body against mine and forcing her tongue deep inside my mouth. Fear had turned to passion in both of us. We necked like teenagers after the prom. I was hoping the wrecker would take its sweet time coming after us.

"There's something I need to say," I said, when we finally came up for air.

"I'm listening."

She smiled, opening wide those dark brown eyes of hers. Her hair was a mess, dirt covered her face, and little beads of blood had formed on her knee. She looked gorgeous.

"I'm not great at relationships."

"What happened between you and Lori?"

"Lori needs closeness. I couldn't give that to her. At least not until after we broke up."

"You still love her."

"Is that a question?"

"No, an observation."

"I guess that's that."

"You barely know me," Connie said, "so you make assumptions. That's a mistake."

"What are you trying to say?"

"I'm like you in a way, but for different reasons. My early existence was very happy and filled to overflowing with family. Great for a kid, but it can be a bit much when you grow up. I became me by leaving family behind. Even in Hollister they were too close. Suffocated me. And there's something else."

"What?"

"I'm younger than you. I'm starting out. I have this apartment in Emeryville, a view of the Bay, swimming pool and workout rooms in the facility. I'm very happy in my own space. I love my career. So right now I'm not looking for the house with the white picket fence and the kids."

"And later?"

"Who knows? I'm not some kind of finished product labeled 'Connie Hernandez.' Today, I want you. Tomorrow?"

"Maybe I'll change in time, too."

"I may not want you to. So let's take it day by day."

I was relieved that she was accepting me as I was, not demanding a commitment that I wasn't ready to make. We had a future. But, I felt vaguely dissatisfied. I wanted her to want more from me. I wanted more from me. But I didn't want to change. As Al Swineheart would say, "Go figure."

I pulled her close and we kissed again. That's when the damned AAA truck showed up.

30.

I heard a slight movement on deck. How had he gotten past my watcher? I knew he would find a way. He was a professional. He had to remove me and then get out of town. Ratto would have insisted. But more. It had become personal for him, just as it had for me. He had to kill me, no matter what the risk.

The hatch cover inched open. A sliver of grayish light entered the *Sea Wolf*'s cabin. The light expanded as the cover slid back. A large shape filled the opening, plunging the cabin again into darkness. He lowered himself down the hatchway. He moved agilely despite his weight.

I saw a red spot bouncing around the cabin. He had a laser light attached to his scope. The spot came to rest on my berth. He had found his target. Three slaps echoed through the cabin. The noise in the enclosed space seemed loud, but I knew nothing would be heard outside the boat.

He walked cautiously past the nav and dinette toward my bunk. He held the Ruger steady, its red spot focused on the mound of blankets. He leaned over to check to be sure he had finished off his victim.

His fist smashed into an object on the berth. He howled like a wounded hound dog. He flayed his hand in the air, trying to free himself. He fell over onto the cabin's floor.

No Time To Mourn

I crawled out from my hiding place among the sails in the fo'c's'le, .38 in one hand and a high-powered Maglite flashlight in the other. I turned it on.

I caught Red's twisted face in a bright circle of light. Ghastly purple hue. Eyes bulging. Wet with grimy sweat. Monty's fangs dug into his hand. Blood dripped onto the floor. Her full seven feet wrapped his arm, chest and neck. She methodically constricted.

"Get this thing offen me," he drawled with a thick Southern accent. "Cain't breathe."

"A word of advice. Never, never strike a Burmese python in the face."

"Cain't..."

"Another suggestion. It is quite useless to wrestle with a python, once she wraps herself around you. She will respond by tightening her grip. Pythons kill by asphyxiation, but I gather you've figured that out."

"I'll shoot if you don't loosen 'im."

He held his gun in his free hand.

"Not if you want to live. Unless I remove my friend Monty from your body, you're going to die. So drop the gun and then we'll have a little discussion."

Red dropped the Ruger. I kicked it away with my foot. I turned on the overhead light. A small tape recorder sat on the dining table. I pushed the "On" button. Then I looked down at Red. Monty constricted with a passion I had never witnessed in her before. Red had really upset her. I would have to make my questioning brief while he still had sufficient breath to speak.

"You killed Susan and Edward Henry."

"Yes."

"Old man was a mistake?"

"Yes."

"You killed Susan so she couldn't inherit the Ratto estate, right?"

"Yes."

"And John Ratto hired you to do that?"

"That what you think?"

"You've got no time for games. It shouldn't take Monty more than another couple of minutes to finish you off."

Red's purple face had contorted into the shape of a gargoyle. He breathed erratically in gasps. His voice was hoarse. I should be feeling sorry for the fellow, but all I could think of was Susan. She had never harmed a soul except for herself through drink. The small window of love and happiness in her life had been brutally closed when this man shot her husband. Then he took what was left of her life. And I didn't forgive him for trying to kill me. Oh, how I wanted to just let go of Monty and watch the bastard die a painful death. But I couldn't. I needed more information.

"Tell you and I'm a dead man."

"You don't tell me and you're a dead man. Die now or later. It's your call."

"Ratto didn't hire me. Imperiale."

"Imperiale?"

"Runs Reno. Movin' into Central Valley farmin' through Ratto. Hired me to find Susan and kill her befo'... Cain't go on."

Red stopped breathing. He really didn't have long to live. I reached down and carefully took hold of Monty's tail. I unwrapped about two feet of her and stopped. This was no easy task. Pythons are essentially long tubes filled with powerful muscles. For obvious reasons, you never unwind a python from the head end. Red began breathing again.

"Keep talking or I'll release her tail."

"Okay, okay. Ratto didn't want to take Susan out. Imperiale insisted. Too much at stake to risk her making a claim on the estate. So when I missed the fust time, Imperiale sent me back."

"Junior was involved."

"From afta' old man Henry got it. Turned out to be a lucky shot. Imperiale figured out a way to use the kid. Put him in touch with me. I used him to set Susan up the night I shot her. Come on, man, that critter's tightenin' again."

"What about Edith?"

"Who's Edith?"

"Junior's sister."

"Don't know nothing about her. Come on, man, that critter's tightenin' again."

So Edward decided to make the call to Edith on his own. If she went to jail, he wouldn't have to split his dad's estate. He might not have even known about the Ratto angle. Nice chap.

I had enough for now on the bastard. I'd let the cops get the details later. In the distance I heard a siren. Nina must be on the way. I had warned her Red would probably show up. I leaned down and grasped Monty's tail with my free hand. I still held my .38 in the other hand. I continued to unwind her.

I had about four feet of Monty unwrapped when I heard the sound of feet landing on the deck. Nina's head and shoulders appeared in the hatchway. She held a regulation police revolver in her hand.

"Looks like you and Monty have got things under control."

"Nina meet Red," I said. "Red meet Detective Peterson."

"Don't' stop now," Red gasped. "Keep on unwrappin'."

"Why don't you put Monty away," Nina said, "so I can come down there? Ollie's out here, too. We have some matters to go over with him."

"Wolf, we'll take charge now," Ollie snarled from behind Nina.

Nina covered Red with her revolver. I placed my gun on the table. I grabbed Monty just behind the head. I gripped her jaws and forced them open, releasing her teeth from Red's hand. Then, I carried her aft and carefully lowered her into her tank. She looked exhausted. But she coiled up, preparing to strike again if necessary. Monty was still pissed.

Nina, followed by Ollie, came down into the cabin. They roughly yanked Red up onto his feet, placed his hands behind his back, and cuffed him.

"What's that mess on your bed?" Nina asked as she looked over the cabin. "Looks like a damned cantaloupe."

"Supposed to be my head," I answered.

Ollie ignored us. He just glowered at Red. He was no doubt wishing for the old days when cops could rough up suspects before taking them in. For once my sympathies were with Ollie.

"Red snuck up on Officer Knowland and shot him in the temple, right through the side window," he said.

"My fault," Nina said. "You warned us. I set it up for Knowland to call in every ten minutes. We were to check him out if he didn't call. I should've insisted on a backup. But I guess I didn't believe you when you were so sure he'd show up tonight."

"He's got a scope with a laser on it," I commented. "And he's a pro."

"Why were you convinced he'd turn up?" Ollie asked.

"I knew Red here was on the run. He would want to get out of the area as soon as possible. He had one more chore before returning to that dirty hole he crawled out of. Right, Red?"

"You all doin' all the talkin' now."

"Don't worry," Ollie said. "We'll nail him through a ballistics match to the murder of Knowland and the other two."

"You'll find a confession on my tape here. He ties in Ratto and Imperiale."

"Who the hell is Ratto?" Ollie asked.

"Susan's half-brother. I'll explain later."

Taking a little card from her pocket, Nina read the bastard his Miranda rights. Then she asked, "Imperiale hired you?"

"That snake of his woulda' made me say anythin'. Now I ain't sayin' nothin' without my lawyer."

"Ollie, let's get Red outa' here and see if he fits into a cell," Nina muttered as she yanked him toward the hatchway.

No Time To Mourn

31.

The air was crisp like a freshly opened bottle of Kendall-Jackson Chardonnay. A slight breeze blew off the San Francisco Bay. Four brown ocean-bound pelicans in formation swept over me. The brilliant luminescence of the sun transformed Jack London Square into a sparkling playland. I could taste salt in my mouth.

Red's hunting ground had become a bucolic scene. The fog had gone. The bleaching sun had blasted away any trace of the blood spilled when Red shot Officer Knowland. A middle-aged boat owner, lugging two sail bags, lumbered down the gangway where I had first confronted Red. A group of four young workers, with identification tags, sat eating lunch in front of the Pavilion where Mildred had charged at me with a broken beer bottle. Azaleas bloomed in window boxes that lined the front of Big Emma's where Red had almost run me over.

I entered the golden incandescent environs of Big Emma's. The joint was nearly empty. The lunch crowd had yet to arrive. Just a couple of PacBell workers who seemed to spend more time drinking in Big Emma's than patching up our telecommunications system. And a half-dozen regulars who, like me, had transformed the place into a second home. I hopped up on a barstool near the door. Lori approached me with a glass of Oban's neat. I pushed it away. Too early to drink.

I filled her in on my hunt for Red in the Hollister area. Then I repeated, almost verbatim, the conversation Connie and I had had as we waited for the tow truck on that lonely road surrounded by apricot trees. Lori sported a bemused frown that evaporated almost as fast as it formed.

"Convenient," she muttered.

I had expected her to be critical of me for not pressing Connie for more of a commitment. What I hadn't bargained for was the sense of relief that broke out on her face. The truth was she didn't really want me to get too deeply involved with anyone else.

I looked up into Lori's eyes. I reached over and grabbed both her hands.

"It's you I love," I said.

"I know."

She burst into tears, fucking up her mascara. She turned and ran down the length of the bar toward the women's room. Everybody stared at her. They were all her friends. Her life. I pulled my glass of Oban to me and took a long drink. Lori returned, big smile on her face, reassuring well-wishers as she made her way toward me.

"Sorry, Jim," she said. "Kinda' messed up my makeup. You were saying?"

"I-"

"I know what you were saying. You know I love you, too. But have you changed?"

I knew she was going to ask me that one. I decided to tell her the truth.

"It's not Connie. She understands how I feel about you. It's me. I feel so damned close to you. Like something has been changing inside me. It should make me happy. Instead it scares me. Murderers are easy to handle. Emotions are another matter. I need my space. Stupid, but that's the way with me. Guess what I'm saying is that I'm still pretty fucked up."

No Time To Mourn

"Maybe I like you fucked up."

She leaned over the bar and kissed me on the mouth. I spotted a tear forming in one eye. Then she smiled her warm smile again and thankfully changed the subject.

"So what happens now?" she asked.

"They've got an iron-tight case against Raymond."

"Raymond?"

"That's Red's real name. Raymond Truett out of Dallas. Known mob connections. The problem will be nailing a slick mobster like Imperiale. The Feds are looking into it under RICO."

"Like the Sopranos."

"More sinister. Tony Soprano is a suburban Mafioso. The Feds think Imperiale fronts for a Harvard-educated, button-down collar syndicate. They launder money for the Russian mob and the Colombians. Then seek legitimate investment opportunities."

"You think they'll really nail him?"

"There's at least a chance either Ratto or Edward will cop a plea and implicate Imperiale. Still, it bugs me. So they lock him up. Chances are the crooked bankers behind him get off scot-free."

"What about the sister, Edith?"

"Made a deal. She's to return the money, pay a ten grand fine, and do six months community service. She's going to be staffing a child abuse hot line. Edith has promised me ten grand for my efforts."

"You know," Lori said, "I keep thinking about Susan. I miss that sad lady."

"I tell myself that I did my best for her. I couldn't prevent her death but I nailed her assassin. Still, it doesn't help. I can't get her out of my mind. A pile of black clothes on a barstool. Lost in drink. That vacant stare of hers. Like headlights that smashed against a fog bank. She was mourning for herself, attending her own funeral ahead of time."

"You should have known Susan when Edward was alive," Lori said. "It was like the difference between Technicolor and black and white."

I took another sip of whiskey and fell silent. There was nothing to say. Lori, as always, sensed my mood.

"You won, Jim. Why are you so down? Couldn't ask for a better day out there."

"Too nice a day. We could use some fog."

The doleful bleating of the foghorn had gone with the fog. No sound cried out to mourn Susan. No gray-white damp shroud awaited her frail liquor-sodden body. Was it time to mourn no more?

"Someone should mourn for Susan," I said, "but I'm not much good at mourning. I have to leave the care of her soul to the Godly. I'm better at vengeance. Wish I had shot Red or at least let Monty strangle him to death."

"That's not nice, Jim."

"It's not a nice world. At least, I caught her killer. I uncovered the bastards that hired him."

"You're weird," Lori said.

"Greed is what makes the system work. Stand in the way of making the big bucks and you get destroyed. Imperiale, Ratto, and Red. They are men of our times. Like the crooked CEOs and the politicians. Susan's the one that just didn't fit. That's what I sensed when I met her. Without wanting to, she got in the way. That's why she ended up the victim."

"Can't save the whole world all at once," Lori said, staring at me with her deep blue eyes.

I nodded.

"So save the world one person at a time. Be satisfied with that."

I nodded again. Then, I paused and reached for my Oban. I took a big gulp.

"Still," I said. "It pisses me off."

The End

Printed in the United States
67189LVS00001B/175